I0784672

J. Allan Dunn

The Treasure of Atlantis

OK Publishing 2021

J. Allan Dunn

The Treasure of Atlantis

Thrilling Adventure in the Legendary Lost City

Published by

MUSAICUM

Books

- Advanced Digital Solutions & High-Quality book Formatting -

musaicumbooks@okpublishing.info

2021 OK Publishing

ISBN 978-80-272-7587-8

Contents

CHAPTER I
THE FLOWING ROAD

"It's good to be back again, Morse, back to civilization, and it's mighty good of you to take me in this way."

Stanley Morse looked at the orchid hunter as the latter leaned forward from the cozy depth of the saddlebag chair and stretched his lean hands to the blaze. The fingers were more like claws than human attributes; the whole man seemed little more than a well-preserved mummy, a strangely different person from the vigorous naturalist Morse remembered meeting three years before on the higher reaches of the Amazon — the "Flowing Road." The man's clothes hung in ludicrous folds about his gaunt frame, and he shivered despite the heat of the blazing logs that almost scorched his chair.

"Nonsense, Murdock!" he said. "I'm only trying to repay your own hospitality. Do you suppose I have forgotten the time you took me into camp on the Huallagos River, when my raft had gone to pieces in the Chapaja Rapids with all my equipment? You've got the malaria in your system yet. Let me get you something to offset that ague."

"It's more than malaria, Morse. There's nothing in your medicine chest, or anyone else's, that can help me."

He laughed a little hysterically and stripped back the sleeve from one arm. The limb, save for its power of movement, seemed atrophied, flesh and muscle and skin had shrunk about the bones until they looked like two sticks held together with twisted cords.

"That's emblematic of the rest of me," he said, as the loose cloth slid back over his knobby wrist. "I've done my last league on the Flowing Road or any other road, for that matter. I've found my last orchid."

"You'll be all right with a few weeks' rest," replied Morse, with forced optimism. "As for the financial end of it, we can build a bridge across that stream."

"I need no man's charity," said Murdock, with a flash of fierce resentment. "If you'll put me up for a while — it won't be long — as you have offered to, I'll accept it gladly; but I can pay my way, Morse."

"That's all right," answered Morse, sensing the excitement of his guest; "we'll not talk of payment. Tell me about your trip, if you feel up to it. And join me in a hot toddy."

He touched a bell, and a deft man-servant answered, retiring to bring in the necessary concomitants.

"This beats chacta," said Murdock, as he sipped the steaming liquid. "And this" — his eyes roved round the big room, the walls set with well-filled bookcases that reached half their height, the spaces above covered with curios and trophies of the chase, mostly South American — "this is a long way from Ucali's hut on the headwaters of the Xingu."

He lapsed into a reverie, staring into the fire, his skull-like head sunk between his hands, as if he could see in the glowing coals the seething cataracts of a torrent racing between rugged sandstone palisades clothed with dense forests, where the lianas writhed between the trees and bound them together in an almost impenetrable jungle.

Stanley Morse, gentleman adventurer, who spent his bountiful income in the exploration of unknown lands for the sheer love of sport and the thrill of danger, watched his guest pityingly. There were hardly ten years between them, he reflected, remembering the man of three years ago, bronzed and lusty, barely entering the prime of life. Now he seemed sixty, twice Morse's own age, and prematurely old at that. Presently he relapsed with a long sigh, finished his toddy, and settled back amid the cushions luxuriantly.

"The headwaters of the Xingu. That was where you came out?" Morse queried. "Don't talk if you are too tired. Let it go until tomorrow, and turn in."

"There may be no tomorrow," answered the orchid hunter. There was nothing morbid in his tone. He spoke cheerfully, as one who recognizes overpowering odds and accepts them bravely. "So I shall talk tonight. Yes, that is where I came out of the carrasco (brush) — alone. But the story I want to tell you begins back of that, on the chapadao (plateau) between the Xingu and the Manoel, south of Para, in Matto Grosso State."

He turned his head, with its dark eyes glowing in deep hollows sunk in the skin that looked like brown parchment, and spoke in a low tone fraught with impressiveness.

"Did you know, Morse," he queried, "that there was a great city on the southern part of the Amazonian plateau?"

"It hardly surprises me," said Morse. "I've never seen any evidences in Brazil myself, but I made a trip to Chan Chan, in Peru, near Trujillo. Pre-Inca they call it. Not much left but a honeycomb of mud walls now, though."

"Mud walls! Pish! I'm not talking of ruins, man! I mean a living city. Temples cut from the living rock, great buildings of stone set along the shore of a mighty lake amid tropical foliage and cultivated fields. Paved roadways, and people thronging them clad in brilliant garments. Boats on the lake, with banks of oars and striped sails. A city set in a bowl of gray cliffs in the shadow of a snow-capped peak with a plume of smoke coming from it like the curl of a lazy fire!"

"You've seen it?"

"Twice!"

He spoke with conviction, and Morse for a moment shared the vision. The next sentence shattered it:

"Twice in the air. Don't think I'm crazy, Morse. It was a mirage, but even a fata Morgana has to be projected from an actual object. And there's tangible proof to back it up. They were not air castles I saw, not the 'airy segments of a dream.'"

Morse tried to veil his growing skepticism. The orchid hunter was Scotch, and the Gaels, he reflected, were apt to be "fey" and see visions. The man was physically and probably mentally sick. But he humored him. "A mirage is an optical effect rather than an optical illusion, I believe," he said. "Undoubtedly there was some solid basis for the reflection. Are you sure about the smoke above the peak? It was my impression that Brazil was free from disturbances. It's a long time since I read up anything about it, but I seem to remember that there were no eruptive features since the Devonian period, according to the scientists."

"A fig for the scientists! Let the scientists travel a country instead of theorizing about it. Show me the scientist who has hacked his way through twelve miles of carrasco and charted the lower Amazonian chapadaos. I lay no claim to being a scientist. I know one branch of botany, but I know it well, and I know enough of geology in that connection to tell a crystalline formation from an amorphous. The valleys of the Madeira, Tapajos, Manoel, and Xingu are floored with crystalline. And the rest of the formations are tilted and faulty. In fifteen years I've known a third as many temblors (earthquakes), and I know a volcano when I see one. Twice I saw it, across the canyon — the temples by the lake, the snow-capped cone, and the plume of vapor. Twice!"

Again he focused his attention on the burning logs, speaking as if the fiery recesses were focal points through which he viewed the strange sights of the land that is bordered by the Flowering Road, the mighty Amazon.

"You know, without my telling you, the general characteristics of the chapadao region," said Murdock. "The main plateaus at an average level of three thousand feet, but up by the streams and rivers into sections, dense forests in the lowlands, woodlands in the shallower valleys, and the grassy campos on the heights. It seemed as if misfortune trailed us. Our bogadores deserted us, the cargadores were a lazy crowd, reports of rare blossoms turned out myths, hardly a week occurred without some accident, common enough, save when they happened so frequently.

"I had started late, owing to difficulties brought up by the European war, going up the Amazon eight hundred and seventy miles from Para to Itacoatiara and so up the Madeira River six hundred and sixty-odd miles to San Antonio Falls. From there I had to traverse and raft it to the Small Pebble Rapid, Guajara Merim, they call it, and it was hard work. I was after a Cycnoches, a weird, night-blooming orchid that looks, by moonlight, exactly like a great azure butterfly. It was worth five thousand dollars to me for every fertile capsule I could bring out, and I stayed longer than I should. It was the middle of September before I started on the four-hundred-and-fifty-mile trek — that's as the parallel rulers mark it on the map — to the Alto Tapajos, with another four hundred miles downriver through almost continuous rapids to really navigable water to Marahao Grande. It was foolhardy to stay that long, but it looked like my last trip with a fortune at the end — and I found my orchid!

"Then the luck turned. definitely. Our stores were low, and we hurried along, half fed, in an attempt to forestall the rainy season. You know what that means — a difference of forty feet in the rivers, making them all but impassable. I never met with such a mat or jungle, lianas fighting us every foot of the way, and the gnats, flies, and beetles, to say nothing of the vampire bats and leeches, draining our strength and impregnating us with their poisons. I had a young chap named Gordon with me. I left him behind, poor fellow! He was a clever naturalist and a plucky comrade. We staggered on, delirious from insect venom often — the whole trip seems a nightmare — and, after crossing the Janiar, the ill luck culminated.

"We came across a settlement where the native chief was sick, and we were called upon to cure him — a common enough occurrence, but one that landed us this time on the horns of a dilemma. The man was dying, due to pass out in forty-eight hours or less, from enteric fever. You can imagine the situation. Fail to treat him, or treat him and fail! It made you either a beneficent wizard or a devil! I did the best I could, and kept him alive a week. He was grateful enough, poor wretch, but there were ugly looks as we left the pueblo, and I knew the news would be sent ahead by the 'jungle wireless,' the hollow logs hung on lianas that they beat with a stick coated with rubber.

"As we advanced, I had evidence of increasing hostility. We had dogs with us, and they constantly warned us of lurking enemies. We extinguished all fires and buried the embers before dark, and all smoking was stopped after nightfall while we kept constant watch. We caught the sound of drums one afternoon, first in one direction, then in another, and I knew we were trapped. The cowardly cargadores started to pick up their packs and flee, but I made them stop, and we felled trees for a barricade. Well, they attacked just before dawn, and poor Gordon was hit with an arrow tipped with urari.

"We beat them off that time, and pressed on, with Gordon in a litter. He lasted three days, with his arm swollen up twice the size of his thigh, and passed out in coma. Four times different bands tried to leave us in the jungle, and each time I lost two or three of the cargadores through flight that undoubtedly cost them their lives. The last time an arrow scratched me, passing under my arm through my shirt. I put leeches on the wound and took strychnine, but I was a doomed man from that moment. My heart failed me at every exertion and the poison was absorbed inevitably into my system.

"We shook them off at last, and two weeks later we crossed a campo of dried grass and came to a great cut in the plateau eroded by a stream that ran in rapids five hundred feet below. I made camp there, hoping to gain strength.

"It was the next morning I saw the mirage. Not I alone, but the half dozen carriers still left with me. It was as I told you, plain in the sky — temples, buildings, lake, boats, and the crowded causeways. I had practically no fever that morning. The cargadores prostrated themselves in terror. That afternoon they left, taking their packs with them while I was having my siesta. My two machete men stayed behind, not from any particular fidelity, but, as they expressed it, we were bound to be killed, anyway, and they might as well stay where they were comfortable and meet death rather than try and run away.

"You may imagine it was not a cheerful situation! I was on my last legs in the heart of the Brazilian jungle, the rainy season close at hand, practically all my supplies gone, without bearers! It was a tight hole. To crown the trouble, the cargadores had taken along my orchids in their scurry.

"There was nothing to do but to make the best of it, and that meant getting under way. My rifles and ammunition were in the shelter, and one of the dogs had stayed behind. There was no use crossing the stream, for the opposing cliffs were sheer and apparently unscalable, though

I thought I saw traces of a succession of rough steps that almost looked like masonry leading to a ledge halfway up the cliff. But there they ended definitely in a smooth wall. So I decided to follow the stream downward. It ran almost due northeast toward the Amazon, and I hoped that later it would widen and become navigable for a raft. Shorthanded as we were, that was a slim chance, but the only one in sight.

"It was useless to follow the carriers. The day was drawing to a close, and I determined to pass the night where we were. At sunset I heard a shout from the machete men, and found them groveling on the edge of the precipice. It was the mirage again, floating in a sky of pale green. It was no hallucination, Morse. I was not the only one to see it, and if ever a man had braced himself for an emergency I was in that condition. I found that the Indians considered it a sure sign of death, a vision of their heaven, I imagine. But the two who stayed with me were real men.

"We struck out early next morning. The plateau sloped sharply downward, and in two hours we were clear of the grass and brush and among trees and jungle once more, following a fairly well-beaten trail. About a mile in, the dog got restless, and we advanced cautiously. Suddenly the hound, which was ahead, began to whimper — he was trained not to bay or howl — and stood still. I crept up to him. The trail widened out. Swinging face downward in the center of the opening, his outstretched fingers a foot clear of the ground, a man hung, one leg caught in the running loop of a rope that was attached to a springy palm, the noose trap that the Indians set for tapirs in the river runways. But this was not a tapir trail. The man had evidently hung there for a long time. The free leg swayed limp, the body was relaxed, and the face, as it swung toward us, was congested. There was a red fillet about his hair that proclaimed him a chieftain, the alcalde of some pueblo.

"We had him down in a jiffy. I could scent help to ourselves from his gratitude if he wasn't dead. We worked over him , and presently he groaned and opened his eyes, and then his mouth, down which I poured some chacta that helped him to tell his story.

"His name was Tagua, chief of a tribe inhabiting the village of Apara. He was an old man, but still too fond of life to suit his nephew who wanted his place. This precious relative had set the trap and then told Tagua that he had seen a tatu (armadillo) on the trail, knowing the old man would travel ten miles to get its flesh. That was the day before. Tagua walked into the trap in the afternoon, and was jerked up in a second. It was fortunate for him that no peccaries came that way, or a jaguar. None of the villagers did. His nephew looked out for that.

"When we had kneaded and rubbed Tagua's joints into place and pliancy, his gratitude knew no bounds. He knew all about us by the wireless drums, and volunteered to send back a message that would leave us immune. He may have given up the information that we were murdered.

"When we marched into Apara, Tagua managing to put up a front for the entry, we created a sensation. Mbata, the nephew, had already usurped the leadership, but he was quickly convinced of his mistaken ambition. After a big feast, Tagua put me up in his own hut, and that night I solidly cemented the friendship. Mbata paid us a visit about three o'clock with a big knife calculated to sever all friendly relations. I woke as he came in, and dropped him with a revolver bullet as he leaned over Tagua, knife in hand.

"After that I owned the village. I had not only saved Tagua's life, but snuffed out that of the one man he was afraid of. He gave me ten of his pisanos (villagers), four of them boatmen and six carriers, and all the yuca, dried fish, and bananas we wanted. More than that, he sent out scouts for my missing carriers, but they failed to find any trace of them.

"I left him my hound and poor Gordon's rifle, with a good supply of cartridges, and he forthwith adopted me. It was not all form, as I will show you. The night before we left, I spoke of the mirage and Tagua confirmed its existence. It was known to his people as Dor, and its inhabitants were not Indians, but men whose skins were white as mine. Long generations before, his people had been used as slaves over a period of years. When the work was complete they had been driven out through a hole in the cliff at the head of the masonry steps I thought I had seen, and the place closed up after them. His own great-great-great-grandfather had been among the captive workmen, and when he left he had stolen a vase from the house of his bondlord.

"This vase had long been a fetish in Tagua's family. It was one of the things Mbata had desired. But Tagua had hidden it cunningly in the floor of his hut, and Mbata had been unsuccessful. It had been a bad fetish, he declared, and to my astonishment, seriously gave it as his opinion that stolen goods never brought good fortune.

"So he insisted on my taking it. And it was gold! He said that twice a year the people of Dor threw many vessels and ornaments of gold and jewels into their lake for sacrifices. The city was sealed in by cliffs that could not be climbed, but it was rich in metal. Gold was used for ornaments, for plates, for drinking cups.

"Whatever his imagination though, the vase attested that he told at least some measure of truth. I took it. We got to the Xingu in the rains, and to Para — "

"And the vase?"

"Is here. I brought it with me."

CHAPTER II
THE VASE OF MINOS

Long after the orchid hunter had gone to bed, Morse held the vase in his hands, turning it over and over while the ruddy firelight played upon the repoussé surface, speculating upon its history. Had he known what the cup held for him of perilous adventure upon the very rim of death, it is possible that he would have resisted the spell it gradually wound about him.

It was untarnished and undented, despite the softness of the beaten surface of unalloyed metal, and it was of the most exquisite workmanship. Finally he set it upon the table beneath the glow of his lamp. The vase was an oval container, exquisitely symmetrical, supported by four serpents of solid gold whose heads met with forked tongues touching beneath the center of the bowl.

Its main surface was divided into two panels by the duplicated design of a double ax. On one side a superbly modeled bull was being baited by a youth and a maid, clad in garments apparently Grecian. The figures were lithe in action, beautiful in pose. Darts clung to the snorting, wounded bull that pawed the ground with lowered head. The other panel was filled with ancient writings above which, in raised letters, was the word minos that Morse easily deciphered, though the characters were ancient Greek.

Here was a riddle: a golden vase brought back from the heart of Brazil, yet eminently Grecian! He turned to his bookshelves, the word "Minos" stirring his recollections. Far into the night he read of the great Minoan dynasty established on the isle of Crete, in the Mediterranean, of its wonderful empire and powerful fleet, houses that possessed ventilating and sanitary systems far ahead of their time, and of the civilization that produced both pictorial and linear writing two thousand years beyond Phoenician culture, for long credited as leader in such matters.

He read of Minos, the Sun God, son of Zeus, and of his wife, Pasiphae, the "all-shining Moon Goddess," of the cruel sports in the Minoan bull rings, the tragic death of Minos, killed by a king's daughter, who poured boiling water over him in a bath. Of Minos' children, Daedalus and Ariadne, noted names of Greek mythology. Of the victims tortured by being enclosed in the belly of a red-hot brazen bull, and of the invasion of the kingdom of Crete two thousand years before Christ, and its final destruction, four hundred years later, in the Dorian Conquest, by the rude tribes of northern Europe.

It was a curious tale, half legend, half history, fancy and fact interwoven in a web of fascination; but what had Crete, the little island empire south of Greece, in common with the tale of Murdock, the orchid hunter, and of Tagua the tribal chieftain over a thousand leagues away, separated by the length of the Mediterranean Sea and the breadth of the Atlantic Ocean?

The puzzle was too great for him to solve. He left it for the time, set back the glowing embers of the fire, placed the vase of Minos in a wall safe, and switched off the lights. On his way to his bedroom, he passed the room set aside for Murdock and smiled at the open door. He knew the sign of the traveler, fresh from months in the open air, to whom closed doors and windows seem to create a stifling prison. As he tiptoed past, he paused to listen to the orchid hunter's breathing. That the man would never travel again the Flowing Road he was assured, and he wondered if his guest was resting easily.

There was no sound. As Morse stood in the doorway, listening, the street lights faintly illumined the room and the prone figure on the bed, fully dressed. It held a rigidity of pose that alarmed him. He entered and bent above his guest, shook him lightly by the shoulder, then raised his arm. The pulse was irresponsive, and the hand fell heavily upon the quilt.

Morse turned on the lights. There was no need for a second glance. Murdock had found his last orchid, had departed on his final trek. Morse telephoned for a physician and sympathetically arranged the wasted form, hardly more than an articulated skeleton.

The orchid hunter had been writing. There was a folded paper beneath a book on the desk that was a part of the room's well-chosen furnishings. This was addressed to his host. It read:

> My heart is very weak tonight. No pain, only an absence of power that leaves me
> barely strength to write these words. I leave the vase and its history, not just in

gratitude, but because I believe it was given me that the mystery of the City in the Sky may be solved. So things work out in the history of us all, I think. The riddle of the race leaves a clew that sooner or later falls into the proper hands. Such hands are yours. Here is my diary, kept daily, and there is a in my trunk that will guide to Tagua and the canyon of the vision.

I have neither kith nor kin. I leave no one to be sorrowful about me save the orchid dealers who made their desk-chair profits from my risks. It was a great game while it lasted, and the Flowing Road is the trail of trails. Good night, good friend; goodby, perhaps, and, if so, remember, when you enter the city of Dor, your grateful visitor,

Ronald Murdock.

The physician confirmed Morse's idea that Murdock's death was not to have been put off.

"Strychnine could hardly have prolonged it," he said after an examination. "It does not need an autopsy to tell that the man's heart was rotten. Valve muscles flabby. He was a strong man once. Urari, you say? Humph! That's a local name for curare, extract of resinous South American barks. Has several alkaloids in its active principle. We really know very little about it save that it is one of the deadliest of poisons. Defies analysis to a certain extent. It must have been a diluted or weakened extract and the slightest of incisions. A friend of yours, Mr. Morse? I am sorry. It was a peaceful death. I will attend to the certificate."

"And I to his funeral," Morse promised himself. A sudden idea struck him, and he registered it as a vow to make a fitting burial of the sturdy Scotchman.

CHAPTER III
LAIDLAW'S THEORY

To Stanley Morse, the dead man's letter, as he read it, seemed to bind him to a quest made sacred by the last testament of the orchid hunter. The more he pondered over the idea, the more it found favor with him. He had no ties nor business to keep him in New York, and the fever of adventure was easily stimulated in his veins. The interior of Brazil offered a trip that he had always promised himself, and the prospects of discovering a hidden city soon dominated both his waking thoughts and his dreams at night.

A week after Murdock's death, he made a visit to the Metropolitan Museum, where he was made welcome by an assistant curator of archaeology. The museum was already the richer for Morse's travels, and he was privileged to ready admission to the administrative offices and the time and knowledge of its experts.

Morse set the vase on the green blotter of the scientist's desk, and, going to the window, raised the blind so that the March sunshine lit the rich metal with a radiance that was dazzling on the high places of the embossed design.

"What do you make of that?" he asked.

The curator took the vase up reverently, examined it with close scrutiny for ten silent minutes, then set it down again.

"Where did you get it?" he parried.

"That is the pith of the story," laughed Morse. "Don't look at me as if you thought I'd been raiding some of your precious cases. I came by it honestly. As a preamble I'll tell you that I'm not going to give it to the Metropolitan or any other museum. It is dedicated to a special purpose."

The official's face fell involuntarily.

"Or sell it, I suppose?"

Morse shook his head.

"It's worth a small fortune," said the curator. "It's a perfect example, a glorious example, of a Cretan vase. The tableau is undoubtedly connected with the Minotaur legend. None of the excavations at Cnossus have unearthed anything finer. Crete, you know, was given autonomy in 1889 by the European powers, and the government exercises a jealous eye over all discoveries. Do you know anything of the ancient history of the island?"

"I've been reading it up of late. I retained enough of my school days to make out the word 'Minos.' What's the inscription?"

The curator shrugged his shoulders. "You'll have to take that to Laidlaw," he said. "I can't decipher it."

"Who is Laidlaw?"

"Gordon Laidlaw, F. R. G. S., archaeologist and anthropologist. Haven't you met him? He's a master scientist, but from my standpoint pretty much of a crank."

"He holds an unprovable theory that the lost country of Atlantis, or its remains, is to be found somewhere on the American continent, where it was left after a mighty cataclysm split the earth into the continents of Africa and America and formed the Atlantic Ocean." The curator spoke almost contemptuously.

"Atlantis? Wasn't there some theory a few years back which tied Atlantis and Crete together?"

"There was a long article in the London Times about six years ago. A man named Martin also advanced the idea. Why?"

"Because this vase was found by an orchid hunter in the center of the Amazonian chapadao, or plateau." "Impossible! I beg your pardon, Mr. Morse, but are you sure of that?"

"Absolutely."

The curator sprang from his chair and paced his office in his excitement, talking staccato sentences.

"It's insane — insane! Can there be something in Laidlaw's theory after all? No, it's preposterous! Atlantis is a myth. A theoretic foundling! And you've never met Laidlaw? It's insane — insane!"

He picked up the vase and fondled it between his palms.

"May I keep this overnight — in the museum?" he asked. "I want to show it to my colleagues and tell them the story."

"You haven't heard it yet," said Morse dryly, "but I'll tell it to you if you introduce me to Laidlaw."

"Surely. He lives up in the Berkshires. I'll wire him. He'll be down in the morning — tonight, if he could get here."

"Will you let me know when he arrives? You have my telephone?"

"Of course. Now tell me about the orchid hunter."

Morse's decorous valet awakened him the next morning before daylight.

"There's a — a person who demands to see you, sir," he said. "Quite an extraordinary party, with a face — you'll pardon me — like a wild lion. Name of Laidlaw."

"Laidlaw!" Morse shook off the filmy net of sleep and set up in bed. "Show him up!" he ordered.

A minute later he heard a bass voice bellowing in the hall:

"Which room? That one? All right."

His door opened as if a gale had forced the lock, and a man, half giant, half dwarf, waddled into the room. Large amber eyes were set in a weather-burned face, as much of it as was discernible in the frame of tawny, shaggy hair and beard that seemed to make up a continuous mane. His nose was beaked like an eagle's, his eyes aflame with a light that might have been equally that of fierceness or a proud invincibility of purpose.

Below the broad shoulders, the massive torso was that of a giant; by all fairness the man should have been seven feet in height, but ludicrous legs, short, curved like those of a Pekingese spaniel, supported the upper frame.

He advanced to the bed, his glance compelling that of the half-awake Morse.

"Where?" demanded Laidlaw, and his great voice boomed like the roar of a bull. "Where is the vase?"

Morse shook off his sleep and slipped on a dressing robe as he rose to greet his visitor.

"The vase is not here, Mr. Laidlaw," he said.

"Not here? You've not lost sight of it? Man, how could you?" The visitor groaned and sat down on a chair where the effect of his dwarfed legs was immediately discounted and he appeared a giant, a troubled giant, mopping his brow and gazing anxiously at Morse.

"It means comparatively little to you, compared to what it does to me," he went on. "I have been scoffed at by my fellows for years on account of a theory that is absolutely sound, but which they smile at to my face and laugh at behind my back, or else say: 'Poor Laidlaw, he's been overdoing things, and he's a bit cracked.' I know them. And now comes the chance to choke them with their own laughter, to make them take back the sneers, to make the most important archaeological discovery of all time — and you've let some one get the vase away from you — the vase that would tell me in a moment whether I was a genius or a crackbrain!"

The man's gestures, the tones of his bass voice, ranging from enthusiasm to deep despair, were almost enough to make Morse laugh. But he hastened to reassure him:

"It's at the museum. I left it there overnight with our mutual friend. I'm sure it will be perfectly safe with him."

The archaeologist groaned.

"We can't get at it until ten o'clock, and it's not yet five! Man! And I've come ramping down from the Berkshires in a rattletrap that stuck in the mud and balked at the hills. Mud up to my waist. I'd have walked to make better time if it hadn't been so deep."

"I had no idea you'd arrive so soon, Laidlaw."

"If you had been waiting for the biggest thing in your life for twenty-odd years, would you hesitate? Though I beg your pardon for letting my impatience upset your household, to say nothing of your sleep."

"That's nothing. You've had no breakfast? I'll order some. In the meantime, here is Murdock's dairy and his map. I'll be dressed before you've read them."

Laidlaw was immediately immersed in the diary. The unconventionality of using his host's bedroom as a reading room did not even occur to him, and Morse smiled to himself at his guest's enthusiasm. He gave instructions for a meal and entered his bathroom. Midway through his shower, the bathroom door opened and Laidlaw's leonine face and massive shoulders protruded through the opening.

"If you've ordered eggs," he said, "I forgot to tell you that I cannot eat them if they're more than just thoroughly warmed through. You'll pardon me for mentioning it."

Morse smiled again before he turned off the shower. The idea of a man who had devoted a third of his lifetime to one theory with an almost fanatic devotion bothering about the time of his eggs was amusing.

"I'm fussy about that myself," he answered. "Always boil them and time them at the table."

"Good!" Laidlaw's eyes roved over Morse's muscular and athletic figure. "Man, but you're powerfully built!" he said. "I wish — but that's one of my faults; I cannot help but envy a well-made man. I've got the torso of Hercules and the legs of a bullfrog!"

He closed the door abruptly and disappeared. Morse began to entertain a singular liking for his visitor with his almost childlike enthusiasm and frankness. Breakfast was over before seven o'clock, and after the meal Laidlaw dilated at length upon his theory of the lost city of Atlantis. The main thread of his belief centered in the migration of the Cretans after the Dorian invasion in the sixteenth century B.C. to a place on the then western coast of Africa.

"All probabilities point to this," he said. "The Cretan, or Minoans, were on most friendly terms with the Egyptians. They were primarily responsible for much of the civilization of ancient Egypt. Their hieroglyphics antedate all others. In Babylonian scripts and many records of Egypt I have found constant reference to Atlantis as a country somewhere toward the west, the setting sun. The Luxor Museum contains a vase and certain inscribed tablets telling of gifts made to Egyptian royalty by the people of Atlantis, and the script and workmanship of the vase are undoubtedly Minoan. Have you a world projection?"

They were in the library, and Morse produced a large atlas, which he laid upon the center table and opened at an equivalent projection in which the world was cartographed in an ellipse. Both bent above it.

"I am only going to take up the question in hand," said Laidlaw, his face lit up with the belief in his theory. "You are, of course, acquainted with the general idea of world subsidence. The Pacific is studded with the mountaintops of a submerged continent, though its depths are far greater than those of the Atlantic. Not a nation or tribe of either inland or coast possessions, civilized or barbaric, but unites in the story of a great flood. This, I maintain, was caused by — avoiding technical terms — a shrinkage of the earth's surface due to the settling of substrata even today manifested in lesser degree by earthquakes more or less persistent along recognized zones.

"Now, look at the contours of North and South America, as opposed to South Africa and Europe. Allowing for lowlands that are now permanently submerged shoals, does not the map resemble a puzzle picture with the assembled portions shaken apart? See how the eastern angle of Brazil, at Cape St. Roque, would fit snugly into the Gulf of Guinea, the bulk of the Sahara Desert lie along the retreating northeastern coast of South America, the lower half of the same continental coast line correspond with that of southwestern Africa."

Morse followed the argument with an interest that began to be leavened by the other. man's conviction. The theory was at least plausible.

"So! Then presume that this cataclysm found the Minoan, then settled in their new country of Atlantis, established somewhere westward of what is now Cape Verde, in the Franco-African possessions. After the movement had subsided, the survivors found themselves on the Brazilian coast, in the neighborhood of Para, south of the Amazon, itself a subsidiary crack of the catastrophe reaching more than two thirds of the way across South America. The sands of Sahara — the sandstone plateaus of Brazil are coeval!"

The idea was startling, revolutionary; yet to Morse, listening to the inspired voice of Laidlaw, it gained possibility.

"But would the Minoans or Atlanteans survive such a catastrophe?"

"Why not? Other tribes did, and handed down the story of the Deluge. There is no reason why their descendants should not be living today. Remember, their have been persistent rumors since the earliest explorations of white-skinned peoples living in the remote interior of South America. If we find a people in Dor who show the characteristics of Atlantis — or Crete — why then my critics are confounded, and you and I will have achieved no small measure of fame.

"What time is it?" he broke off.

"Eight o'clock."

"I can't wait two hours, Morse. It's an impossibility. Where is your telephone?"

He called the assistant curator at his home and persuaded him to meet them at the museum within half an hour. Falling in with his mood, Morse brought his car around and within a quarter of an hour they were standing on the steps of the Metropolitan, with fifteen idle minutes facing them. Morse lit a pipe and watched Laidlaw curiously. The latter paced up and down with the nearest attempt to a stride his ridiculous legs would permit. It would be a rash man, Morse thought, who would make open fun of the scientist's physique. The mighty chest, and arms that swung below the knee, the leonine face, eagle nose, and keen eyes held a promise of more than ordinary strength that would easily offset the handicap of the bowed, short legs. Laidlaw might lower the pace on a trail, but he would be a good man to have along in a pinch.

The assistant curator appeared at last, stepping down from a bus and blinking through his glasses. Laidlaw waddled down the steps, clutched him by the arm to the amusement of the passersby, and almost bore the slighter man up to the museum entrance, not releasing his clutch until after they were in the department office. Then he spoke for the first time.

"The vase?" he gasped.

"If you'll let go my arm," said the curator, with mild reproach, "I'll get it out of the vault."

Laidlaw mumbled an apology, and the museum official departed, rubbing his almost paralyzed arm. When he returned, he handed the vase over to Morse, who in turn handed it to the expectant Laidlaw.

The theorist trotted to the window with his prize like some great mastiff with a bone, and examined it minutely, inside and out, from all angles. There came a series of grunts from him that Morse translated as both favorable and excited.

"What did the museum authorities think of it?" he asked the curator.

"Cretan, beyond a doubt. You will pardon me, Mr. Morse, but our experts are inclined to believe some extraordinary coincidence must have taken that vase to the Brazilian jungle. Some Old World adventurer, who carried it with him on all his journeys. The other suggestion is — appears to be — inexplicable."

Morse shrugged his shoulders.

"It is interesting," he said. "I am going to see what there is in it. I have always intended an expedition into the heart of Brazil."

"Is Laidlaw going with you?"

For the moment Morse was frankly at fault. Then he laughed.

"To tell you the truth, I had never thought of him as not doing so. Since he arrived at my house before daylight there has been little doubt of his determination, and he apparently took it for granted that I agreed with him. Even if I had not practically planned the trip, Laidlaw has a certain way with him. . ."

The curator nodded.

"Most fanatics have a gift for persuasion. . .But I shouldn't call him that. He may be right. Who knows?"

And then, changing the subject: "Mr. Morse, the faculty has empowered me to make you a very liberal offer for the vase. It should be preserved for science and the public benefit — "

"If it passed from me to the museum it would be as a gift," said Morse. "But that is impossible."

"As a loan? While you are absent?"

"I'll tell you what I'll do," said Morse jestingly. "If you think you can get it away from Laidlaw, I might agree. But seriously, it may be useful on the trip. I want to take it along, and I have decided to dedicate it to an object that is more or less sacred to me. If we get through and back again, I'll bring the museum something that will more than make up for it."

In the meantime, Laidlaw, his face aglow, had left the window and seated himself at the desk, entirely unconscious of the presence of anyone. Vase in front of him, he was copying the characters of the script onto a pad, evidently intending to waste no time in deciphering them.

"He'll do in a few minutes what would take us hours," whispered the curator to Morse. He is the acknowledged authority on Minoan lore for all his tangential ideas."

They watched him working energetically, arranging the symbols, grouping and comparing them. Presently, he laid down his pencil with a sigh and gazed into vacancy, exaltation irradiating his strong features.

Morse and the curator moved toward him. He regarded them blankly; then recognition slowly came into his eyes.

"There," he said triumphantly, "is a literal translation of the linear script. No doubt Mr. Morse will permit photographs of the vase before we take it with us. There is no time for confutation before we start. It is up to the museum to verify this translation and to prepare the world for what will come out of Brazil. Listen!

> Minos Son of Zeus and Europa Minos the Sun God.
> Husband of Pasiphae The All-Shining Pasiphae the Moon Goddess.
> Father of Ariadne The Exceeding-Holy Ariadne the Nature Mother. Minos the King The King of Kings Minos the Law Giver.
> Made by Zal the Artificer in the forty-ninth generation after the Great Flood in the seventh year of the reign of the Fifth Pta, descendant of Minos, King of the New Atlantis in his capital of Dor.

Laidlaw brought his great fist down on the oak desk with a shwack that splashed the ink from the wells.

"Ha!" he exclaimed. "Refute that if you can. The forty-ninth generation after the Great Flood in the reign of the Fifth Pta, King of the New Atlantis! The gift vase in the Luxor Museum bore the name of Pta the First."

He turned to Morse.

"And I am taking the glory," he said. "It is you who have solved the matter. Wherever the name of Laidlaw is mentioned, that of Morse must be coupled with it."

Suddenly his exultation faded, and his face grew anxious. "Mr. Morse," he said, "I have been carried away by my own enthusiasm. I have thought you shared it. You have been so interested, so cordial to me, a — crude and blustering fool who broke in on you like a thief in the night. I have assumed you were going to Dor. It is your discovery; I have no right to exploit it without your permission. I understand you are an explorer, that you know much of South America — "

"Say no more, Laidlaw. I am going to Dor; I have a mission there aside from the adventure. You will join me, of course. You are a scientist; I am merely an explorer, and an amateur one at that. It would lend me dignity if you were to go along."

The face of Laidlaw cleared and he gripped Morse's hand silently, his features working in their emotion.

"There is one condition," said Morse, as he released his fingers and slipped his hands into his pocket.

"Anything. What is it?"

"That you reserve your handshakes for your enemies, not your friends. I won't be able to hold a pen for a week."

CHAPTER IV
CAXOEIRA CANYON

Vivid flashes of forked lightning, following hot puffs of wind, illuminated the aisles of the Amazonian forest, inky black between the intervals. The long line of carriers, tired of struggling over and under the tough festoons of tree roots and ground vines and the trailing lianas that disputed every inch of the trail, came to a sudden halt. The two leaders, stumbling persistently behind the bearers, confirmed the move, and the Morse-Laidlaw expedition tried to find secure shelter from the coming storm that had driven night before it in such untimely fashion.

There was little cover from the threatened hurricane that could be considered satisfactory. The cargadores threw their burdens beneath the heaviest undergrowth they could find, and, with their employers, leaned against the tree trunks. Morse and Laidlaw ensconced themselves in a fold of a great massaranduba (cow tree) as the first heavy drops fell.

"I'm not built for this trail, Morse," said Laidlaw, though his cheery voice evinced no complaint. "I've tripped up in these infernal jungle traps a dozen times. My nose is bleeding, and I've cracked both shins falling on my rifle."

"And I've been swung off my feet with a noose about my neck about as often," replied Morse. "We're due here till morning, anyway. By tomorrow night I hope to reach Apara. Here it comes!"

They shrank against the mighty bole as the gale swept through the forest, the roar of the wind intensified by the crackling of trees that were literally up-rotted and tossed by the tempest as if they had been so many wisps of straw. Two trunks crashed down close to their feet, and only the giant spread of mighty bough above them saved them from destruction. In the intermittent pauses of the storm the shrieks of monkeys and the screeching of parrots and herons joined the wailing of the bearers and machete men in an appalling din. Birds flapped heavily to the branches overhead; animals shuffled in among them; and once a wild cry of dismay went up as a great snake wound its scaly length among the Indians, too disturbed for attack.

The gale lasted two hours. It was the last effort of the rainy season, and had not been unexpected by Morse, who had deliberately chosen the time of the trip to take advantage of the high water in the rivers. They had come by steamship to Para, at the mouth of the Amazon, traversed eight hundred and seventy miles of the Flowing Road to the mouth of the Madeira, and ascended that tributary nearly seven hundred miles in a launch to the San Antonio Falls, above which the river raged in continuous rapids for three hundred miles, impossible for upriver travel. At San Antonio, they engaged their porters and machete men and struck eastward across the great plateau broken up into subsidiary chapadaos, crossing the Tapajos River at Taguaraizino, and its tributary, the Manoel, at the border angle of Para and Matto Grosse States, reaching the old, half-grown trail of Murdock, and arriving with a few days' march of Apara village, at a stream marked on the orchid hunter's map as Caxoeira, in the beginning of May, with six months of good weather in prospect.

It had been a hard trek, and the caravan showed signs of the trying-out process. Morse had marveled at Laidlaw's adaptation to the trying conditions. Once eggs disappeared inexorably from the menu, he made neither murmur nor suggestion as to meals, accepting chameleon or monkey with manioc for vegetable and banana for dessert with equanimity. The drawback of his short legs was eliminated by his endurance.

Once, for sport, he had drawn himself up into the lianas and swung along above ground for a hundred yards as easily as a gorilla, scaring the prehensile-tailed monkeys that chattered above him and striking awe into the hearts of the Indians. The quest well started, nothing seemed to disturb a certain humorous equanimity that characterized him and made him an ideal trail companion. Torrential rains soaked them; they steamed in their own perspiration; gnats and gaudy-flied, heavy-shelled beetles, all laden with poison sacs and natural hypodermic syringes, tormented them, but they proved immune to the fevers, and their formidable numbers and equipment secured them from hostile attacks.

Morse was in top condition. By dint of strict discipline and a general knowledge of conditions, he kept his train in similar shape, and they made unprecedented time. Across the grassy summits of the chapadaos, the day's march was more often over than under twenty miles, and a general spirit of confidence in their own ability permeated the party. Morse had said nothing to the bearers concerning the real object of the expedition. He had consulted with Laidlaw, and they had decided to keep silent.

"We may not be welcome at Dor," Morse suggested, "and, according to Murdock, the Indians seem inclined to be superstitious in the matter. We don't want to lose them before we reach Apara."

In spare hours since they had left New York, Morse applied himself, under the tutelage of Laidlaw, to acquiring facility in ancient Greek and learning to decipher the symbols of Cretan pictorial and linear script.

"There will be variations in the language, undoubtedly," said Laidlaw, "but the roots may be the same, and present practice will prove a fine working basis." So Morse resurrected the memories of his school and college classics and pounded away until he was able to converse freely with Laidlaw. Except where the Greek held no equivalents for the names of modern articles, they practically adopted it in place of English.

"Dialects spring up and mother languages alter with change of location and climate, much as we will undoubtedly find the old Cretan ceremonials and customs, religious and social, dominated by local conditions," warned Laidlaw. "If the snow-capped cone mentioned by Murdock is a volcano, it will undoubtedly have had its influence on their worship. The old Minotaur legend will likely have become a myth unless they have cattle, which I doubt. The volcanic fires will have an important part in their ritual, I imagine. Though it is, of course, all theory on my part."

With education and speculation, the time passed quickly, and it seemed only a short time since Laidlaw had first burst into Morse's bedroom. A genuine friendship, founded on mutual peril and respect for each other's bearing and sturdy manhood, sprang up between the two men. Morse was amazed at the resources of Laidlaw's learning, and Laidlaw treated the other as a son of whom he was justly proud, relegating to him the leadership by right of experience and capability.

The morning after the storm, Morse broke camp at daybreak. The hurricane had blazed a broad trail of uprooted trees, torn undergrowth, and lianas through the forest and strewn it with boughs and branches. Dead birds lay here and there, and one great limb had smashed to a pulp a great anaconda fully thirty feet in length and as thick around as Morse's thigh.

According to the map, they had crossed the last watercourse and had now only to climb out of the valley to the highlands where Tagua ruled the village of Apara. During the morning they made good progress, and at sunset they arrived at the village and sent in word to its ruler with gifts of bright-colored prints.

There was no surprise at their appearance; the jungle wireless had announced them as it had elsewhere along the route. The bearers fraternized with the half-naked pisanos of the village, and two headmen escorted Morse and Laidlaw to a large bamboo hut which they speedily made comfortable with their camp equipment.

Morse asked for Tagua by name. "Tell him," he said, "that we are friends of Murdock to whom he made the present of the cup of gold."

The response from the chief took initial form in return presents of fat capybaras, an agouti, and an armadillo, together with wild figs and bananas. In half an hour the chief arrived, apologizing for his delay. He had been in a mud bath for his rheumatism, and had waited to cleanse himself. He limped badly, and was evidently in pain, though he beamed with evident friendliness.

"You come from Senhor Mirradoche?" he asked in the flowing Indian dialect. "Does he send greetings?"

"Greetings from beyond the trail, Tagua. The senhor is dead."

"Eyah! It is bad news. He was a good man. I linger like an old tree, but he is taken."

He lapsed into silence which the Americans did not interrupt. At length he asked: "What may I do for you?"

Morse repeated the story told by the orchid hunter.

"We would find the city and enter it," he concluded.

Tagua sank back in mingled incredulity and horror. "It is impossible!" he exclaimed. "The way is closed, and they permit no strangers within the city save as bondmen. You cannot go alone. And none of the pisanos would dare go with you. It is a land of ghosts who dwell sometimes on the land and sometimes in the sky. Have I not seen it? Did not Mirradoche see the Sky City and the people walking?"

"Nevertheless we will go," declared Morse, "even if we go alone. Where is the way?"

"You are strong men and brave," said the chief thoughtfully, "and friends of my friend. Therefore I warn you. But you men of other jungles are all mad and most stubborn. Yet, maybe you are magicians. Have I not heard of him who swings in the trees and talks to the apes like a brother?"

It was somewhat of an exaggeration; but Laidlaw, who had long ago mastered the key language of the Amazonian dialects, laughed.

"But that will not help you scale the walls," Tagua went on. "The way leads by the stairs that Mirradoche told you of, but they are broken and the ghosts have sealed the cliff. Give it up, senhors. Maybe tomorrow you may see the Sky City from the campo. I myself will lead you opposite the stairway. Then return while still your bodies hold your soul."

They quizzed him, but he could add nothing to the dim legend that once the Indians had been forced to work in the Land of the Ghost People and had been driven out at the end of their task, his ancestor bringing with him the golden vase he had taken.

Morse opened a pack and produced it, setting it on the camp table. A cover for the vase had been made at his direction, carefully designed to conform with the original. This was soldered tightly to the bowl.

"This cup," he said, "was given me by our friend. In it are his ashes. I shall give them burial within the city of Dor. I swear it!" he added, setting one hand upon the urn.

Tagua looked at him with astonished admiration.

"If you say so, then I believe you will do it."

Outside the hut, the night was filled with weird noises when they emerged. Tagua had declared a feast in his visitor's honor. Fires blazed at the ends of the mud-caked street, and villagers dressed in gaudy prints, bedecked with strings of alligator teeth, feathers, and lustrous bird skins paraded up and down behind musicians beating loudly on drums and blowing piercing notes through reed flutes in rude rhythm. With them mingled the bearers and machete men. Native liquors were in evidence, and the crowd sang and danced at will.

At the appearance of Tagua and his guests the crowd entered a big hut decorated with fresh palm trees and lit by tallow dips along the walls. The chief conducted Morse and Laidlaw to a platform at one end to watch the dancing, which took place on the uneven mud floor with much stamping of feet to the drums and flutes. It was evident that before long the native ferments would be in full possession.

Morse took advantage of the first pause brought about by temporary exhaustion and stated the object of the expedition. With the first mention of the Sky City a silence fell upon the mob. He concluded with a call for volunteers, promising a rifle to each man and other rewards that would make them comparatively rich for life.

The men shuffled their feet and whispered among themselves, and Tagua spoke.

"I am old and useless," he said. "Also I am afraid of the Ghost People. Yet would I go with these two if only that shame should not be set upon my village and Apara be called the abode of cowards. Maya" — he singled out a tall warrior hung with rows of alligator teeth — "what say you?" The men stepped forward. His chest bore the scars of close encounter with some sharp-clawed jungle denizen; he carried his head high, and was evidently regarded as a sub-chief.

"If I send an arrow against a jaguar or a man," he said, "I know when I have hit. If I miss, it is my fault. But how can one fight against ghosts when the arrow pierces a shadow and is lost in a cloud? Yet am I no coward. What one dares I dare! Xolo! Will you follow these strangers with me?"

Xolo, long and lean, streaks of gray in his black hair, not an ounce of spare flesh on his body, naked save for a breechclout, corded with stringy muscles, came to the side of Maya.

"I will go," he said simply.

But that was the end of the recruiting. The men who had accompanied the expedition were paid, and neither Morse's offer of high payment nor Tagua's persuasive powers could coax another warrior into service. Maya and Xolo were the best hunters of the district, Tagua said, and both had performed notable deeds in war against hostile tribes. Better still, while both were adepts with spear and bow and blow gun, Tagua had intrusted them from time to time with the use of the rifle given him by Murdock, and they were accustomed to its use and fairly good shots.

It was not Morse's idea to make an entry into the mystic city with any force that might be construed as an attempt at invasion, but he had hoped to secure enough men to bear the bulk of his equipment. With only Maya and Xolo available, he and Laidlaw were forced to spend the morning reducing their outfit to only the most necessary articles. The two Indians were intrusted with rifles; Morse and Laidlaw, besides these, armed themselves with automatic pistols. A few presents, a compass, powerful flashlights, some few canned provisions, with ammunition, made up the bulk of what they selected to take with them.

The rest Morse gave into Tagua's charge.

"If we do not return for these before the rainy season, they are yours," he said, after opening one bale that contained cotton goods of startling color and design, which he gave outright to the chief.

They set out in mid-afternoon for the spot where Murdock had camped across the canyon from the stone steps. Tagua accompanied them. Close to sunset they came out of a clump of carrasco upon the edge of the precipice. The wall dropped almost sheer five hundred feet to the torrent, which, swollen by the recent rain, swirled and seethed from bank to bank. The opposing cliff was far higher than the one they stood upon, a perpendicular scarp of rock on the rim lifting up to almost a thousand feet.

The setting sun was almost level with the flat summit of the plateau behind them and painted the farther cliff with a broad band of rose. Beneath their feet the canyon was in shadow, in which the foaming rapids showed like a cavalry charge of gray horses.

Morse imagined that he could dimly make out the stone steps leading halfway up the cliff. Laidlaw was gazing at the summit of the opposing wall, sharp against the eastern sky of pale turquoise-matrix green, flecked here and there with little rosy clouds, the heralds of the gorgeous afterglow to follow.

Suddenly he drew in his breath sharply, and Morse looked up. Tagua, Maya, and Xolo were on their hands and knees, their heads resting on the ground.

In the sky, ethereal, slightly tremulous, but distinct, was the vision of a city built upon the shores of a lake that held the reflections of its stone buildings and of colonnaded temples that seemed to be hewn out of the solid rock. On the lake, ships were being rowed shoreward with banks of oars, some propelled by sails of striped material, a multitude of people were passing along a paved highway by the edge of the water. Luxuriant verdure set off the buildings, and, reared from the back cliff, there rose a snow-capped dome with a plume of smoke lazily curling from its peak.

As the sun dropped behind the western edge of the plateau, the colors of the mirage blended with the afterglow, the waters of the lake seemed to slowly rise and inundate the city, the plume of smoke became a floating cloud, and the vision vanished.

Morse and Laidlaw turned in common impulse and clasped hands. There was no need for words. It was the city of Dor, cloud-painted indeed, but a sky canvas copied from an original that lay somewhere beyond the high precipice that now bent a grim frown upon them, the rosy band vanished with the descending sun.

CHAPTER V
KIRON

Morse and the scientist were on the canyon rim before sunup, but no mirage greeted them. Evidently the vision occurred only during certain atmospheric conditions. To both of them its timely appearance upon their arrival seemed a happy harbinger. But, as they gazed into the depths of the gorge, evidence that the real difficulty of the quest was just making itself manifest was very clear.

In the still morning air the hissing rush of the turbulent waters far below them was plainly heard. The descent from where they stood appeared impossible, nor, as far as they could see in either direction, could they determine any natural trace of a trail. In the present high condition of the water, the torrent lapped either precipice without indication of a beach from which to launch whatever craft they might use in crossing.

Opposite the stairway, which led only to a narrow ledge, the Caxoeira surged in a great whirlpool, part of the giant eddy evidently occupying a hollow in the cliff directly below them. As they gazed, great logs came riding down the current, tossed about like matches in a mill stream, rearing half their length out of the wild race of tawny waters as they struck against submerged rocks, plunging, splintered and sullen, back into the tide to be carried on the circle of the whirlpool till they were sucked into the vortex or spurned from the outer eddies into the main current.

"We'll have to wait a day or so until the water goes down," said Morse. "We could get down the cliff with ropes, but to cross that flood is a different proposition, even if we had a raft ready built and at water level."

Laidlaw shrugged his shoulders resignedly.

"I suppose so," he answered, scanning closely the stairway with his binoculars. "There is no doubt but that has been built up with a masonry of boulders and cement," he said. "But either it led to a higher ledge which has fallen away, or Tagua's story of the opening appears to be sheer legend. I can't find a sign of any entrance, past or present. But it must have been built for some purpose and led to or from somewhere."

Tagua had returned to his village the night before, and neither Maya nor Xolo could offer any enlightenment. Maya volunteered the information that the stream was fifteen feet above its usual height and might be expected to return to normal within forty-eight hours.

"But the whirlpool," he added, "is always present."

A mile upstream, the cliff could be descended to a stony beach as soon as the water subsided.

"We should find plenty of stranded logs to make a catamaran," said Morse. "We can use lianas to bind it together. They are even better than rope. And we'll need poles and paddles." He gave the order to Maya and Xolo to descend to timber level and secure these, with sufficient green lianas, when Laidlaw, who had continued his examination of the stairs, grasped his arm and drew him back from the brink of the cliff, motioning at the same time to the Indians to follow the movement.

"What is it?" asked Morse. Laidlaw's face was flushed, his eyes blazing with excitement.

"Crawl out to the edge, and you'll see," he answered, setting the example.

Flat on their stomachs they cautiously moved to the brink, Maya and Xolo wriggling behind them like snakes.

The face of the cliff that backed the ledge to which the stone steps led was no longer a blank wall. In it appeared two openings, symmetrical, equal, evidently the work of man, separated by a narrow strip of rock that protruded like a tongue across the ledge.

"A slab that swings on a pivot," muttered Laidlaw in Morse's ear. "Worked from within only, in all probability. But an entrance nevertheless. Look!"

The word was superfluous. The attention of the four pair of eyes was glued to the openings not far below their own level. Through the righthand portal came a figure, clad in a loin cloth of red and yellow stripes, fringed to the knees. A short cape of jaguar skin hung over one shoulder.

In one hand he bore a long wand tipped with metal. His skin was copper-colored, but worn and weathered like some piece of driftwood from the sea. Through their glasses, Morse and Laidlaw saw, with growing eagerness, that the man was an Indian, but unlike any they had ever seen.

Laidlaw's hand rested on Morse's shoulder, and his powerful fingers sank deep into the latter's muscles. Four more Indians issued from the heart of the cliff. These wore only short clouts of yellow. Between them they bore the naked figure of a man, bound with arms tight lashed to his sides, the ropes encircling him to his ankles so that the body was stiffened with the wrappings. His skin was in marked contrast to the others. Where the sun had not tanned it, it was white.

Through their glasses they could see the man's lips move, though the noise of the river drowned his words. His face was calmly contemptuous, the features regular, the hair smooth and dark. His captors made no attempt at answer, but laid him down on the ledge, helpless. The man with the staff bent over him and ordered some loose boulders to be set between him and the rim of the ledge. Then he motioned to the others, who preceded him into the dark mouth of the tunnel. Ten seconds after their disappearance the slab turned on its pivot and fitted into the cliff so completely that the powerful glasses failed to reveal a trace of its existence.

Morse sprang to his feet, followed by Laidlaw.

"He's not an Indian," he cried.

"He is a Greek, distinctly a Greek," said Laidlaw.

"Whatever he is, we've got to get him off of that," said Morse, and suddenly cupped his hands and shouted. The man, by frightful effort, had succeeded in slightly arching himself upon the soles of his feet and the top of his head and was trying to edge himself to the verge of the narrow platform.

"He can't get by those boulders," said Laidlaw. "That's what they put them there for."

"I'm not so sure of that," replied Morse. He's making a desperate attempt. He didn't hear me. I wish we had a megaphone. You try it, Laidlaw. Tackle him in Greek."

The next instant the scientist's stentorian voice bellowed its message. It bridged the noise of the stream and the bound man turned his face toward them as Laidlaw repeated his brief sentence of friendship and promised help. A slight smile passed over the man's face, but he renewed his efforts, only to abandon them temporarily from exhaustion.

"He understands me, I am sure of that," said Laidlaw. "But he seems bent on killing himself. I wonder what he's afraid of?"

The question was answered by a shadow that slid over the ground among their own. Looking up, they saw a great bird soaring in the blue. Higher up was another speck, and beyond that yet another.

"Urubu," said Maya briefly, as the vulture planed downward in a great spiral.

"That's what he's afraid of," said Morse. "Before we could reach him those brutes will strip his bones. I imagine he's afraid of losing consciousness; and they may not wait until he's dead, seeing him helpless. He prefers a quick death to a slow one. Well, we can discourage their little game."

The scavenger of the sky wheeled so close above their heads that they could feel the draft from its outspread pinions, the naked, repulsive neck craning from a ruff of dirty white feathers, its eyes regarding them curiously but unafraid. Laidlaw raised his rifle.

"Better wait till he lights and make sure of him," said Morse. "And look out for a — "

"I'll leave it to you," said Laidlaw. "You're the better shot. But don't leave that poor devil down there in suspense, tortured like a modern Prometheus."

The vulture suddenly lifted his wings tip to tip and dropped plummetwise to the ledge, where he spread his pinions for balance, losing all the grace of his early motion as he shuffled along the ledge toward the helpless man.

Morse's rifle cracked. The bullet thudded softly into the broad back of the bird between its shoulders, and with a harsh croak it toppled from the ledge and fell into the whirlpool, a lifeless bundle of feathers.

"Next!" said Morse grimly, levering a cartridge into position. Another vulture hovered uncertainly above the canyon, and, gaining courage, made the ledge, only to meet the fate of the first bird. A third, realizing that unusual conditions prevailed, halted on the topmost rim of the cliff, peering over until a bullet settled him.

"You'll kill the bound man from fright yet," said Laidlaw, "to judge from his face. He must take us for gods."

"That's a dangerous role to adopt, from all I've seen," said Morse. "I don't see any more of the brutes about. I fancy we've accounted for the local air patrol. Now we've got to get across to him somehow. He must be in torture from those ropes. Tell him we're coming, Laidlaw."

The scientist roared his message across the gulf, and the man nodded. Apparently the summary slaughter of the birds inspired him with confidence in the men who spoke to him in his own tongue, for he ceased struggling.

"Now then," said Morse, "we've got a man-size job ahead. Let's get at it, Maya!"

The Indians disappeared on the run, and Morse and Laidlaw overhauled their store of strong hempen line, set aside some provisions, and cached their rifles and the remainder of their goods in the thick brush, retaining only their automatics. Maya and Xolo returned with a supply of lianas and half a dozen stout poles which they had trimmed with hand axes. There was no time for shaping paddles, and Xolo explained that they would not be necessary. He studied the whirlpool intently, and Morse passed his field glasses for better observation. With a brief grunt at the power of the lenses, Xolo continued his survey of the eddies for several minutes.

"I think," he said, "there is a big cave below — so." He scooped out an imaginary hollow with his arms and squatted on his haunches. "We will make a raft and find the current." He traced the proposed course with his finger in the soil. "If we keep close into this side, we will follow the water to the other. Then Maya and I will jump ashore on the steps. There is a big rock there for anchor."

Even from the height it seemed a desperate venture, but Morse knew the skill and knowledge of the Indian raftsmen, and their two companions were superb examples of courage and strength. Gathering up the equipment, they followed Maya to the point where he declared descent was practicable. It was a hard climb, encumbered as they were, with sheer descents from ledge to ledge, but they accomplished it at last and stood on a great, level-surfaced boulder a foot above the rapids.

Xolo took the hempen lines they had brought and busied himself in the manufacture of a lariat, while Maya carefully surveyed the preliminary eddies. Speech was only possible by shouting above the thunder of the raging water, racing by with tawny manes, fretting at the rocks that curbed its mad career to the Amazon, a thousand miles away.

The Indian poised himself, his fellow standing clear of the whirling loop, holding with Morse and Laidlaw the slack of his line in readiness to take up the sudden tug. A log came riding down the cataract, its heavier butt lifting the lighter upper half. Xolo tossed the lariat, and the noose settled fairly behind the projection of a broken branch. The swift pull almost dragged the four men from the boulder before Morse could snub the line about a smaller rock and bring the log to rest alongside their impromptu wharf.

In half an hour they had secured six fairly matched logs and dragged them on the boulder. Then they set to work to make four of them into a rude platform, binding them together with the lianas. Laidlaw's strength was a notable aid in hauling tight the lashings. The two remaining logs they arranged as outriders, rigging them with some branches that the current had already washed among the rocks. When it was completed they were smoking with perspiration and ready for rest and food.

"We'd better strip, Laidlaw," said Morse, as they finished the meal. "We may stand a better chance if we have an upset."

"Small chance of getting free of that maelstrom," said Laidlaw, as he began to peel his sweat-glued shirt from his massive chest. "What do we do?"

"We'll fend off when we're told," said Morse. "Otherwise we'll leave it to Maya and Xolo."

It was hard work to launch the catamaran, which, the moment it was freed, was swept away in the clutch of the current, bucking like the craziest of wild horses. The Americans knelt for steadiness; but Maya and Xolo, balancing themselves, rode the writhing logs upright, one at either end of the raft. Their judgment of the swift surges was marvelous, seeming to see the hidden rocks as plainly as if the torrent bed was dry, while thrusting with their poles and avoiding a dozen disasters in a minute, and keeping the catamaran close to the nearer shore. In five minutes they had entered the whirlpool, and the hollow predicted by Xolo showed in a deep cavern swept by the tawny, foam-streaked waters. The rocking logs, threatening every instant to tear away from the tough web of the lianas, were sucked under the cliff by a force that seemed bent on smashing them against the inner wall.

"Yai!" shouted Xolo, and Morse and Laidlaw thrust with all their might. The stout poles bent like bows, and Morse felt his muscles cracking with the strain, while Laidlaw's stood out from the mighty shoulders like clustering snakes. A second more and they were free of the hollow and riding the circumference of the whirlpool in a great arc toward the opposite shore and the stone staircase. Xolo crouched for his leap and sprang, his bronze body lithe as that of a jaguar, carrying a line with him which he quickly cast about the boulder he had noted from the clifftop. Maya followed with another line, and slipped on the wet surface of the rock, falling waist-deep into the torrent.

For an instant the raft swung to the single line, taut as a harp string, opposing the full force of the current. Maya, clinging with one hand to his rock, pitched the line he still held to Xolo, who took two swift turns about the boulder. The double cable held. Maya scrambled ashore, and Morse and Laidlaw followed in safety just as the first line parted with a twang. The raft swung broadside and the second line, chafing against a sharp surface, gave way. The logs, suddenly released, entered the whirlpool at a tangent and were rapidly drawn into the vortex, disappearing in a broken jumble.

"Touch and go, Laidlaw. There goes the grub!"

"How do we get back?" replied his companion with a grin. "If I wait till that stream goes down I'll be too weak to wade, much less swim."

"We won't go thirsty, anyway," answered Morse. "Where's that bundle?" He looked for a special parcel of restoratives bound tightly with the lesser lianas that he had tossed ahead of him. It had dropped safely on the surface of the steps, and he picked it up.

The lower treads of the stone stairway — and they were obviously cut by human hands — were submerged. The remainder led steeply up the side of the cliff, broken away here and there, but easily surmountable.

The party hurried up them to the ledge where the prisoner lay. As the four came into sight of the bound man, they stopped dead in their tracks. Close by the prostrate form poised a great vulture, beak ready to plunge into the unprotected man's face.

Morse's pistol flashed from its belt holster, and the foul creature fell, flapping feebly, across the form of its intended victim. Laidlaw, as swiftly as his short legs would allow, reached it and flung it by one wing far out into the canyon.

The man had fainted. Maya and Xolo slashed at the leather strips that had sunk cruelly and deeply into his flesh, while Laidlaw chafed the released limbs with gentle strength and Morse forced a few drops of aguardiente between the clenched teeth. The man swallowed, coughed on a second mouthful, and opened his eyes upon the solicitous face of Morse upon whose knee his own head rested.

"We are friends," said Morse in Greek. For a second the man's eyes looked puzzled, then he smiled and answered in a swift gush of words of which Morse only vaguely caught the drift. Laidlaw answered promptly, and the two began an animated conversation which Morse interrupted by an offer of iguana flesh and bananas which the man gratefully accepted.

"You'll soon get the swing of what he says," Laidlaw told Morse in English. "The language was certain to. have some variants, but essentially it is the Greek of Homer. I will ask him to talk more slowly. He has said that we are not friends, but his preservers — gods, in fact. I am trying to disabuse him of that idea."

When their patient had completed his meal, Laidlaw looked whimsically across the scraps at Morse. "I wish I were a god," he said. "I wouldn't be so dependent on food. You haven't got a banana or two hidden away for supper have you?"

The two Indians had taken over the rubbing of the Atlantean's limbs, massaging them methodically, apparently a little in awe of him. He accepted their ministrations as one born for such attention.

Presently he stood up and stretched himself, going through a series of calisthenics that he persisted in despite his evident stiffness. His body was as finely modeled as a Greek statue, muscles showing evidence of athletic training, ivory skin speaking eloquently of special care. Beside Laidlaw he appeared almost a stripling. The Atlantean was more a reduced replica of Morse's almost perfect physique.

As the twilight gathered in the depths of the canyon, and the setting sun painted its daily band of rose on the cliff above their heads, he told his story.

"I am Kiron," he began, with a proud consciousness of all the name imported among his own people. "Male regent of the New Atlantis. In the one hundred and twenty-third generation after the great flood" — Laidlaw looked meaningly at Morse — "the last Pta died without issue, and the people were divided concerning a successor. So the kingdom was made a double kingdom, and a son and a daughter of the two brothers of Pta were made joint rulers. Ever since then a king and queen have reigned over the land together. Now, Rana, daughter of my uncle, is queen. She is ambitious to establish an individual monarchy, both from her own desires and those of the priests under Ru, who is their chief.

"Rana is not my consort, for it is against our law for the children of brothers or sisters to mate with each other. Neither is there love between us; nor has there ever been. Moreover, my heart is long given elsewhere.

"Therefore, she and Ru plotted against me that Rana might rule, for there is no one of the rank to take my place. Open warfare they feared lest the best of the land be killed. For you must know that we people of Atlantis mingle not with other nations, and much care has been given to our breeding that the race might sustain its strength and beauty. It is the law of Atlantis that none may lead who are not perfect in body. Indeed, despite all care in mating and the development of the young men and maidens, we have lost much in stature."

He paused and gazed admiringly at Morse.

"There goes any lingering idea of my godhood," said Laidlaw. "I don't qualify."

Kiron resumed his tale. "Rana and Ru sent me a message to come to her in secret on a question of grave import. When I did so, they commanded me to be seized and borne to this place by the secret way that has been closed for many generations, leaving me here for the vultures to devour.

"It was a shrewd stroke. I was at my private palace of Zut, and crossed the lake by night — last night — and none saw my entrance to the palace by the royal water gate save my slaves. I found Rana and Ru, and their henchmen made me captive without preamble. No others know what has befallen me, and Rana and Ru would not dare announce it. For I am beloved of my people.

"They brought me here at daybreak, and as the bird-settled for its meal — you came! Henceforth you are as my brothers." He extended his hands to them with a gesture of equality.

"Will not your slaves tell of your visit?"

"All Atlantean slaves are bred dumb," Kiron answered. "Neither can they read nor write. We find that it makes them far less prone to revolt. . . It is a good custom." He looked casually at the two Indians, squatting apart, and they seemed to catch the import of his words.

"Now, my brothers," said Kiron, "tell me of your purpose and of your own land, in which doubtless you are princes."

Laidlaw complied, Morse listening with increasing ease as the familiar accents of the scientist's voice aided him to catch the change of phrasing and of word endings. The scientist dealt lightly with American customs and democracy, and soon included Morse in his story with the discovery of the vase. Kiron's interest evinced itself by his rapt silence. Night fell as Laidlaw told of his own researches in Europe and northern Africa, of his theory and its apparent proving.

The stars came out and the shining constellations changed as they swung above the canyon gap, but Laidlaw still boomed his tale in sonorous Greek.

They were three thousand feet above sea level. The night was warm and two men, one naked and the other practically so, listened to a third, whose mighty upper body showed gray in the dusk, tell his strange story. The two Indians, smudges of silent statuary, hunkered with heads on their knees, appeared to sleep as Laidlaw knitted together the raveled web of bygone ages and annihilated the years, while below them the torrent labored at the never-ending task of world-shaping.

"By all the gods, that is a mighty tale!" said Kiron. "And you may hold me witness that it is the truth. As prince regent, I was taught much of our lore that is hidden from all save the priests and monarchs, and your story bridges the chasms and throws light upon the dark places. Ru shall hear you and be abashed before your knowledge, and all Atlantis shall proclaim your wisdom."

He turned to set a friendly hand upon Morse's arm.

"And you, brother, who are formed even as Minos himself, son of Zeus and god of the sun, greatly will we reward you. And, because of your manhood, Atlantis shall make you a first noble and you shall enter the Brotherhood of Kal."

"You do us honor," said Morse. "But how may such things be accomplished? It seems to me we sit outside a barrier beyond which lies your kingdom and the fulfillment of your wishes toward us."

Kiron laughed. "Truthfully," he said, "I had forgotten. On the third morning slaves will come to find what the vultures have left and cast the remains into the river, and then report that Kiron has been disposed of. We will stand aside until the way is open, and it shall be the slaves who are fed to the water. If you care not to soil your own hands, I will slay them with mine."

He spoke with an arrogant confidence in his powers. "So we shall descend the pathway of the burned out fires and come to Dor," he continued. "It will be a rare sight, the faces of my Cousin Rana and of the high priest, Ru! They will say nothing, for even Rana's people would not,. dare to seize me and would rise against her. A king of Atlantis may not be judged save by universal consent. You will do well to watch Rana's face, my brothers. It is as beautiful and yet as cruel as the Flower of the Long Sleep that slays you as you bend to inhale its fragrant, deadly breath.

"But where is this vase you speak of?"

"It is across the canyon with the rest of our weapons and some of our supplies," said Laidlaw, sighing half out of weariness and half out of hunger.

"We may cross the river by nightfall tomorrow," said Kiron. "I fear I have left you hungry, yet what is hunger compared with the gain of knowledge and of friendship? Let us sleep here on the ledge. Tomorrow we shall pass to your encampment and return to punish the dogs that Rana intrusted with her treachery."

Morse spoke to Maya and Xolo and, without a word, they found a sleeping place and settled themselves for the night. The Americans and the Atlantean were soon to duplicate their example.

They cat-napped away a good part of the following day, with some time devoted to fruitless exploration. In the late afternoon the torrent had subsided sufficiently for them to cross the stream, wading and leaping from boulder to boulder, and to climb to the summit of the cliff.

While Maya and Xolo prepared the meal that was so badly needed, Kiron examined the vase.

"It is from the royal treasury," he said, "though the cover is of strange craftsmanship. See here the double axes of Minos and Pasiphae. I would like to meet the dog who stole it!"

"He is long since dust," said Morse, and he explained to Kiron the presence of the funereal ashes of Murdock within the vase and his intentions concerning their disposition.

The idea caught the young king's imagination. "It is a worthy deed," he proclaimed. "It shall be carried out, and the name of your friend carven upon the walls of the temple along with your own. Have you not brought great news to Atlantis?"

After the meal he examined with unconcealed wonder the rifles, the field glasses, compass, and chronometer, following intelligently the explanations of Laidlaw of their use and mechanism. The compass was new to him only in form. The flashlights excited his particular delight. "They are little suns," he exclaimed, "little suns that shall light us through the fire path."

They recrossed the stream with little difficulty in the gray of early morning, relying on Kiron's assurance that the slaves could not reach the ledge before dawn. Carefully and quickly they disposed themselves close to the gate that led to a lost race.

The sun rose behind the cliff, touching the plateau with a glorious golden color. The Indians were motionless statues on the stairway. Morse, Laidlaw, and Kiron stood quietly against the cliff on either side of the opening. Time passed slowly.

Suddenly, without a sound, the great slab of basalt swung upon its pivot and ears strained for the footfalls that must follow. Out from the dark hole came the leader, advancing onto the ledge with the staff that proclaimed his authority held firmly in one hand. The silent watchers did not move. Now, four men appeared in the opening and their emergence became a signal for action.

Silently, on the balls of their feet, the three attacked from behind. Morse felled the nearest with a single blow and Laidlaw's fist crashed down upon the back of another's skull. Both fell, blood gushing from the mouth of the one the scientist had hammered with his great fist.

The headman sprang backward, whirling his staff in both hands as Kiron ran in upon him. The Atlantean ducked under the weapon and seized his opponent around the hips. Without apparent effort he raised him and heaved him over the cliff as if the powerful slave leader had been an inanimate bundle of little weight.

One of the slaves fled down the staircase, only to meet the charging Indians. In an attempt to stop, he lost his footing and plunged into the gulf below. The last man fought furiously, but Laidlaw gained a gorilla-like embrace and quickly pushed his crumpled opponent away.

Before they could interfere, Kiron had spurned one of the fallen slaves over the precipice. His fellows lay insensible. "We shall leave these carrion to the birds."

"Let your little suns shine," he said, "and I will lead you to Dor."

CHAPTER VI
THE GATES OF DOR

For a little way the tunnel was dimly lit by the daylight that came through the opening. Kiron reached above his head and tugged at a bronze handle attached to a lever working in a slot of metal in the wall. A sound of falling water came to their ears, and the daylight faded as the gates behind them closed upon the outer world.

"Hydraulic?" asked Laidlaw.

"The lake has thrice risen and flooded the lower dwellings," said Kiron. "The engineers drove a course-way through the rock that follows this tunnel and empties into a great cleft we shall presently cross. The flood waters open doors automatically and carry off the waste. Meantime we use a small supply to open and close the gates and raise the bridge."

Morse used only his flashlight, saving Laidlaw's and the extra batteries for an emergency. The power lens and reflector gave a brilliant light that was amply sufficient. The way led slightly upward through a shaft of volcanic origin. The flashlight revealed iridescent walls that occasionally changed in character, though always carrying the scars of ancient fires. At times great stalactites hung from the roof, and once they walked through a realm covered with the yellow prisms of sparkling sulphur crystals. The steamy air was laden with brimstone. Laidlaw, testing the water that trickled down the sides, hastily withdrew a blistered finger.

To right and left, chambers and passages opened out. The floor had been roughly paved, and their progress was rapid. Ten minutes' travel brought them to the cleft which Kiron had spoken of. Here, the sound of rushing waters beneath them could be plainly heard. But the gap was almost entirely covered by a bridge of bronze cantilever construction. The heels of Morse and Laidlaw clanged on its metal, and Kiron, once across, pulled another handle. The bridge swung upward on silent hinges, completely blocking the passage and leaving a deep gulf in front of it.

The tunnel showed increasing signs of man's work. Its steeper pitches had been made into series of low steps. At regular intervals along the sides, bronze brackets connected with an ornamental pipe that seemed to be designed for lighting.

"They are served from metal reservoirs at the far end which contain a gas that collects in the fissures of the mountain," explained Kiron. "The control is at Dor, and they are only lit on special occasions."

"There is volcanic fire also?" asked Laidlaw.

"Dor is beneath the shadow of a great volcano in which lava simmers," answered Kiron. "And in the temple, below the Spot of Sacrifice, is a deep shaft in which the fire of the altar of the gods always plays. Tele, the astrologer, whom you shall meet, will tell you that the wrath of the gods has not been manifested for more than fifty generations. Our traditions tell us that New Atlantis was born of fire and water, and by water and fire it shall be destroyed."

Presently the tunnel became quadrangular with smooth walls and ceiling. Frescoes appeared, painted upon a plaster background with occasional bas-reliefs in the same material, showing rows of processional figures treated in the style of decorations found in the ruins of early Greece and Egypt.

Before one of these Kiron halted while Morse turned his light upon the pictographs. They represented an enormous creature, seemingly as large as a hippopotamus in proportion to other figures. It stood erect on hind feet, balanced by a great tail, it sides covered with scaly armor. Parallel lines of servants and warriors in crested helmets, with broad-bladed swords, framed the monster. On one side was the giant form of a man with the head of a jaguar, holding a bow, the arrows from which bristled from the chest of a great beast. Above was a cartouche filled with hieroglyphics which Laidlaw translated.

"Here Pta the King, Pta the Hunter, Pta the Lord of All that Breathes, killed the Beast of the Caves. Mighty is Pta!"

Laidlaw waved his hands excitedly. "The beast is a mylodon, one of the mammoth cave sloths of the Pleistocene and recent deposits. A fantastic find!"

"Its skeleton and skin are in the royal museum," said Kiron. "It is said that this was the last of its kind, but in the last three generations there have been reports that a great beast lives in the big caves at the southern end of the lake. What truth there is in this I do not know, but I have often meant to hunt it. If you wish, we will some day seek the beast together. Those death-giving tubes of yours should be more than a match for it, and you shall gain the wreath of victory."

Realizing that the king was offering them an honor coveted by himself, Morse thanked him. "Let us teach you the use of the tubes, and you shall not be outdone even by Pta himself."

Kiron remained silent, but his expressive features could not hide the pleasure that came to his face.

Abruptly, the tunnel turned to the right. They mounted a long flight of steps with daylight far above them. At the head of the staircase the way was closed with massive bronze gates, and beyond there loomed a beautifully paved terrace guarded by a balustrade of stone. Beyond this, traced against a cloudless sky, were the serrated summits of a volcanic ridge.

A circular gong of bronze, three feet in diameter, hung close to the gates. Beneath it, in a wall niche, was a knobbed stick, the end thickly coated with rubber. Kiron picked it up and handed it to Laidlaw.

"Strike, my brother," he said, "and strike your mightiest, that Dor may know a king knocks at its gates. But strike only once. Kings summon with one call, one stroke, one trumpet cry, and others knock and wait."

Kiron's nakedness had been covered with a long strip of striped cloth from the Americans' supplies. It was draped about him and belted to form a flowing skirt that fell halfway between knees and ankles, making a mantle that covered his shoulders and left his right arm bare. Xolo had made him a pair of sandals from broad forest leaves such as he himself wore.

Morse, watching Laidlaw grasp the rubber knob, smiled to himself at his companion's soiled and stained khaki, the trousers tucked into high, laced boots, a dingy solar helmet upon his head. He became aware of his own disarray and wondered briefly how this lost people might regard their travel-worn appearance.

Laidlaw swung his arm, and the rubber knob struck its target fair in the center. It tilted heavily at the ponderous blow, and the deep cry of its vibrations echoed in the tunnel and beat against their eardrums.

The sound had not reached its height before a man in a short skirt and a jacket that resembled a bolero appeared. The surprise upon his face changed to consternation as he beheld Kiron and the strangers. For a moment he hesitated in apparent bewilderment.

"Open!" pronounced Kiron somberly.

The man produced a curiously pronged key, inserted it in the lock, and turned it. As he pressed his foot upon a metal stud in the paving, the gates rolled noiselessly aside. The man groveled.

"Pardon, O great king!" he stammered. "I had thought — "

"Let it be your last one," said Kiron sternly. "Thoughts can be dangerous at a time like this. Send quickly and bring us litters.

"It would be better, I think," he said, as the man disappeared at a run, "if we go in closed litters to my wing in the palace. There we can attire ourselves fittingly. You will permit me to offer you clean linen?"

Morse accepted, pleased at the Atlantean's delicacy.

"Give me a long robe, Kiron," said Laidlaw, "that these legs of mine may not too early disgrace your standards."

"Would that mine bore as stout a body," replied Kiron. Then he continued: "The rains are over, and this is the month of Minos, the festival month of the reappearance of the Sun God. At noon, when he looks through the roof of his upper temple, the people will assemble and give thanks. Ru will address them and doubtless Rana will as well. She may lament my absence," he added satirically. "I shall be glad to be on hand to reassure her."

By this time three litters of carved wood inlaid with carved ivory panels on which the double ax was conspicuous were at hand. Morse and Laidlaw climbed into two of these, and pulled close the silken curtains at Kiron's direction. The strong shoulders of the bearers took them along in comfort.

Lying on his side, Morse could observe the lake through a crack in the curtains. Stretching toward purple hills, the water was dotted with islands. On the nearest one rose the white columns of a temple surrounded by trees. Boats with striped sails glided over the water.

The lake seemed to occupy the bowl of a great crater. Its waters were strangely blue and placid; the blue of another world. Off in the distance came the distant sound of trumpets. A deep-throated chant echoed mournfully across the water. But no one was encountered, and the bearer's feet padded along tirelessly in route to their unknown destination.

They entered a doorway and traversed a passage lined with white stone on which the double-ax sign was endlessly repeated. Finally, the litters were set down, and Morse and Laidlaw stepped out into a paved courtyard in the center of colonnades.

Palms grew in great vases between the pillars. The bearers disappeared noiselessly. Kiron stood beside the edge of a pool in which a fountain splashed in the sun.

"Welcome to Dor!" he greeted them. "I will show you your apartments; my own slaves will attend you."

He led them to a room of great size. The walls were frescoed in gesso duro, with unglazed window openings cased in bronze lattice, over which trailed flowering vines. Low couches and chairs shaped to the figure stood about. Through a doorway they caught an inviting glimpse of water in a pool.

Kiron pointed to another door of paneled wood.

"There is your bath," he said. "When you have bathed, will you join me in the pool?"

Morse gazed in astonishment at the lavatory fittings.

"Hot and cold water!" he exclaimed. "Silver fittings, ivory combs! And a mirror, no less!"

He surveyed himself disconsolately in a tall plate of polished metal.

"A nice pair of scarecrows we are!" he said. "Fine visitors for a palace. Look at this luxury, Laidlaw. You take it as if you had registered at the Ritz."

"I expected it," said Laidlaw. "The Cretans were fully our equals in sanitary science. Thank the Lord for a bathtub. I wonder when we eat?"

"You're impossible," laughed Morse. "What do you think they'll serve us? Peacock and mullet, I suppose. I'm hungry myself."

A series of light knocks sounded on the door.

"Come in," called Laidlaw.

A pair of bronzed youths entered. One bore a ewer of gold in a deep bowl in which snow was closely packed with two goblets inserted bowl downward in the cool crystals. The other carried linen cloths and a cake of what might have been soap. They retired without uttering a word.

"Kiron's silent system," commented Laidlaw. "I wish this soap-weed cake were edible."

"What's in the pitcher?" asked Morse.

"Try it." Laidlaw poured the silver cups full of a ruby-colored liquor that smelled of spices and grapes. It was sweet, cloying to their palates, but nonetheless invigorating. After a hot bath, they crossed the main apartment to where Kiron awaited them.

Without a word, the three moved simultaneously, diving into the inviting, emerald water and racing for the far end of the marble tank, a hundred feet away. Just as the fingers of Morse and Kiron were outstretched to touch its side, Laidlaw, with a mighty surge, forged in ahead of them, the winner of the undeclared race. More youths awaited them as they emerged, dripping, clad them in loose linen wraps, and escorted them to couches. There they were massaged with sweet scented oils. A servant brought a pile of garments, dividing them into three groups. The youths assisted Morse and Laidlaw to invest themselves in the strange attire, after one had passed a comb through Laidlaw's tawny hair and beard, to his passive disgust. Kiron and

Morse were shaved quickly and smoothly by attendants with wedge-shaped razors that were as well-tempered as any American product.

Laidlaw was garbed in a pleated skirt of dull red that fell to his insteps and was bordered with a fringe of gold. His misshapen dwarf legs were well concealed. A golden girdle, scaled and flexible as a snake's skin, held it in place. Above was a tunic of fine wool, purple in hue, the left arm short-sleeved and the right bare, showing Laidlaw's Herculean proportions to their full advantage. Gilded sandals, bound with thongs of soft leather, and a fillet of the same material about his brows completed the costume.

Like some lord of ancient Assyria, he walked the length of the pool, squaring his shoulders before the critical eyes of Kiron.

Morse wore a double chiton of white wool, sleeveless, caught at the shoulders with gold fibulae brooches, and belted with vermilion leather incrusted with gold filigree set with pale-green olivines. The skirt of this singular garment touched his knees, and its cloth was bordered with golden brocade. His sandals were scarlet, his garb almost a duplicate of Kiron's.

Morse enjoyed the freedom and coolness of the costume, and his naturalness brought an exclamation from Laidlaw.

"You look like an Atlantean to me, Morse."

The discarded clothing lay on one of the couches of the main apartment when they entered. Kiron showed them a space in the wall, masked so cunningly by a part of the design that the uninitiated eye would never suspect its existence. In it they stowed their goods, and Kiron revealed the secret of its opening by pressing the paneled eye of a big cat creeping over ivy-covered rocks and about to spring upon a pheasant-like bird.

"Now," said the Atlantean, "let us eat. We have an hour before the middle day."

Laidlaw did not try to suppress a sigh of pleasure.

In the courtyard, a trestle table and seats had been arranged. Glossy leaves bearing red waxen flowers were entwined between goblets and platters of gold on a white cloth. The peacocks of Morse's imagination did not make an appearance, but the mullets were typified by a lake fish of delicate flesh, served in a sauce of thyme and cucumber. This was followed by a pudding of meal, surrounded by a number of enormous frogs' legs. A sweet pudding filled with chopped fruits ended the repast, at which time even Laidlaw attempted to loosen the links of his girdle.

There were litters in attendance, and the three were borne from the palace behind silken curtains. When they halted in a paved alley between high walls, Kiron dismissed the bearers and led the way to an entrance barely the height of Morse. The Atlantean struck his foot upon a disk of metal that protruded slightly from the threshold, and the bronze gateway slid into the wall. Fifty steps stretched down to a corridor leading to a blank wall. A flower of bronze, hollow-centered, projected from a stone slab.

Kiron advanced and spoke into the petals. Immediately there was a light sound of clicking. A section of the wall descended into the floor. Kiron turned his head to Laidlaw.

"We, too, have our inventions," he said proudly as they passed through the opening. "This is a hidden entrance to the temple."

A long incline appeared before them, rising to the antechamber of a great hall, and ending in a high screen woven from golden threads into a weird design of foliage and fruit. The workmanship was so fine that the light pierced it, and through it came the sound of a high, querulous voice.

"That is Ru," said Kiron, anger rising in him.

A blare of trumpets followed; a burst of voices in a swelling harmony. A strange incense penetrated the antechamber. A woman's deep contralto, ineffably sweet and alluring, reached them.

"Re has removed the veil from his face and smiles once more. Great is Re. The blossoms are invested with his breath and speak of golden fruit. The land sends up incense. The hearts of youth listen to the mating cries of the birds and are glad. Atlantis smiles beneath the glory of Re that now descends upon us."

And now a chant sounded:

"His glory descending Our hearts fill with pleasure Our voices ascending In manifold measure Proclaim adoration,

> The joy of a nation To greet thee, O Re!
> Re! Re!
> Giver of Light and Life!
> Our hearts with joy are rife,
> Hear us, O Re!"

Beyond the screen, the hall was suddenly flooded with a golden glow. Presently the woman's voice broke the silence.

"The golden flower opens! Lo, our prayers are acceptable! Gladness shall come to Atlantis, and fertility. Yet there is a shadow upon the radiance that showers down. Kiron, our king, beloved of Re, is missing from the festival, absent from this gathering."

A cry arose of "Kiron! Kiron!"

But Kiron did not move, and a sardonic smile crossed his face.

"Wait! Rana has not yet ended."

"You call for Kiron, and he answers not," said the queen. "Some grave misfortune must have befallen him. The oracles are silent, though Ru, your spirit lord, has besought them. The holy fires smoldered sullenly at his questioning."

"Kiron! Where is Kiron?" called a voice, quaveringly. "Has he lost favor with the gods?"

"I cannot answer you, my people," said Rana. "Like you, I can only ask: 'Where is Kiron?'"

"Here!"

Beckoning Morse and Laidlaw to follow, Kiron strode around the screen. Bearded priests in flowing robes encircled a platform. A slender woman stood before a throne of gold that glittered with gems. Beside it, a second royal chair was empty. The emblem of the double ax, gleaming blades on ebony staffs, loomed between them. From an opening in the roof, a shaft of sunshine poured in. Beyond it the Americans vaguely glimpsed a multitude of shifting forms.

"Here!" repeated Kiron, one arm upraised, advancing until he stood in the center of the dancing motes of sunray. "Kiron is here, and unto Re the Sun God gives his salutation."

A cheer from a thousand throats echoed from roofs and walls.

Morse saw Rana shrink back, terror in her eyes. A priest whose robes were heavy with brocade down which his long beard broke in a silver shower stepped to her side and whispered. She straightened her slim length and advanced to the edge of the dais. Her eyes were transformed into crimson orbs of hate, which she quickly masked with lowered eyelids.

"Zeus be praised!" she said. "Kiron, chosen of Re, Rana the queen rejoices with our people."

She extended a hand that was like a white flower. Kiron chose to ignore it and ascended the platform as the people roared their approval.

"People of Atlantis," he began, "I bring to you my brothers, strangers who are not strange, visitors who bring tidings from the remote past, of Minos, king of kings, bearers of great news. See, Re shines on them and hails them as his own!"

The shifting shaft of sunbeam had enveloped Morse and Laidlaw where they stood.

"Disperse to the feasting and the dance," said Kiron. "Presently Ru, high priest of Minos and of Re, shall address you. We would be alone with our new brothers."

Morse and Laidlaw felt the challenge of keen glances. Morse found the gaze of Rana directed at him with an admiration that she made no attempt to hide. Laidlaw's amber eyes encountered another kind of look. For there was both challenge and threat centered in the narrow look of Ru.

As the crowd departed, Kiron addressed himself to Rana. "The vultures feed on the carrion you sent to give them daintier food. Are you not glad to greet me, cousin?"

"You speak in strange riddles, Kiron," she answered softly in a voice that held the magic of united strings. "Truthfully, I am glad to see you. Present me to your brothers."

After his one speech to Rana in which he acknowledged her treachery, Kiron, strangely, made no further mention of it. To Morse's astonishment, he spoke to his cousin in a cordial and open manner, as if the subject were forgotten.

Kiron occupied his throne, settled himself naturally, and directed Laidlaw to relate his story to the ring of priests. Rana, in the meantime, had beckoned Morse to her side with a slight motion and a strange magnetic look in her deep and unfathomable eyes. In spite of his knowledge — and he could not shake the picture of Kiron lying bound upon the ledge as food for the vultures — he felt an attraction to this beautiful woman. He fought it wonderingly. Rana was beautiful by any standards, and her manner was an entrancing combination of swiftly changing vivacity and languor. Insensibly Morse began to place much of the blame of her actions upon Ru, who made no attempt to hide his antipathy for the strangers, even as he acknowledged the wonder of Laidlaw's story.

The ring of priests stood wide-eyed as Laidlaw told of the discovery of the cup, and showed keen interest in his account of the island of Crete and its history. There was unbridled enthusiasm at the disclosure of a living race who were at least remotely related to them. And there was wonder and disbelief as Laidlaw promised to display a collection of photographs of Greek art and architecture, the American describing as simply as he could the nature of a "sun picture."

Ru listened with a scowl deepening on his brows, alternately watching Laidlaw and Morse, or noting the satirical smile that continually played across the face of Kiron.

Rana plied Morse with a thousand questions, and her expressive eyes and red, pouting lips were a magnet to him. "Were there many men like him in his own land? Yes. Ah, he was surely too modest. In Atlantis such a man might aspire to anything; even a throne!"

Morse, in almost a hypnotic trance, tried to affect an ignorance of her plain speaking. She halted and appraised him, a trace of puzzlement on her brow. And all at once the vivacity flamed again. She covered him with a flattery that made no attempt to hide her delight in his person. She praised his Greek and promised to be his personal tutor of Atlantean idioms. She outlined a tour with a score of things to see with her as guide. And she made it clear that any attempt to include Laidlaw would prove distasteful to her.

"Let him prate to the priests," she said. "He is old and I do not like his legs." Evidently her keen eyes had judged their hidden proportions, despite the long robes. "His face is hairy, and he is a musty creature. Knowledge is for age, when the joys of manhood are mere fruit husks. Let us not waste our time upon rinds when the luscious pulp is before us."

At last Laidlaw was finished, but there was further talk with the priests. There were games in the afternoon, and what better time was there that Ru might present the strangers to the people?

"He can sit in the priests' benches," said Rana, indicating Laidlaw. "You shall sit with me."

Somehow, the imperiousness, the totality of her manner began to penetrate his consciousness, and beyond the outwardly beautiful shell he began to see her more clearly. Morse began to wonder what her purpose was in showering him with attention.

He was limp and perspiring when he left her spell; aware that he had been fighting with himself for nothing more than his own right to think; aware of her beauty and her magnetism; and suddenly and vividly aware of how Kiron had been tied and left to die at her command. He shuddered.

Laidlaw was full of talk and excitement. He was in his element. He had talked past a meal and had not even missed it. Now that the great archeologist had a few minutes apart from this hidden people, he could not silence his hoarse voice. And while he had been addressing Morse all along, he suddenly realized that his fellow American was there.

"The queen is a beautiful woman," he began, a question in his voice.

"She is that," replied Morse unfeelingly.

"Remember Kiron," admonished Laidlaw, for once laconic.

Morse nodded slowly, and was silent for a time.

"There is something about her," he said at last, searching carefully for words. "When she was near me it was almost as if that part of me that knew what she had done was blocked out — there was something powerful about her. . . She is powerful!"

"Ru is powerful, too," said Laidlaw. "He hates us, and someday he means to fill a throne. If that day comes . . . " Laidlaw stopped and drew a finger across his throat suggestively. Then he continued:

"The old struggle between church and state is here. And the Atlantean priesthood is losing its grip. The people are overcivilized, too sophisticated. They demand to be amused, and the theologians are unable to satisfy them. Ru recognizes this and realizes that his only way of retaining power is to seize the throne. Oh, I found out a few things," said Laidlaw. "Didn't talk all of the time!

"Kiron is a cultured aristocrat, the kind out of style in most of the world. He was born to privileges that he will not give up lightly. Rana is a woman. One thing only dominates her — sex. It is her weapon, her armor, her delight; the one thing that Ru plays upon. He has her convinced that Kiron's indifference is scorn, and she hates him.

"Ru has no love for either of us, but he fears you because you could become a permanent fixture — if Rana can dominate you."

Morse looked at him quizzically. "You seem to have a keen insight into the ways of women."

"I? Risk myself in that kind of labyrinth?" Laidlaw laughed, but there was a touch of bitterness in his voice. Morse wondered whether there was a claw mark somewhere that had not entirely healed.

"Rana," summed up the scientist, "has been spoiled by adulation. As princess and queen, she has been accustomed to cry for the moon and keep on crying until she got it. Now that she's in power, she is incorrigible."

"Don't you believe in suffrage, Laidlaw?"

"Suffrage and sex — the fair sex don't make a team. Over there" — he pointed to the island they had seen from the litter where the columned temple rose from its setting of tropical verdure — "is the home of Atlantean suffrage minus sex. It is the island of Sele, inhabited by a cult of women who have deliberately subordinated sex to the pursuit of knowledge and power. Their leader is none other than Rana's sister, Leola, who is said to be more beautiful than Rana herself. But Rana is not jealous. Leola abjures mankind. She is the high priestess of Pasiphae, the moon goddess, sharer of the double ax."

Morse looked at the island with curiosity. An island of beautiful virgins who had deliberately chosen to challenge men's prerogatives was intriguing to him.

"Only the priesthood is allowed to land there," said Laidlaw, interpreting his friend's glance. "Ru and his followers are also celibates. I don't imagine that Leola and her followers are over-popular. The population of Atlantis is on the wane."

"Do you think they have any chance of achieving their ambitions?" asked Morse.

"To become the equal of man? I doubt it. Mentally and physically they are handicapped by the sex instinct. It would take many generations to overcome that, and by their own laws future generations are impossible. They can only add to their numbers by fresh recruits who are largely influenced by the chance of becoming more or less conspicuous. The priestesses of Pasiphae are very important at festival functions."

"If you had been Adam, the world would never have been populated," laughed Morse. "Eve would have had a lonely time of it."

"It is because there is some of the old Adam in me that I am on my guard," replied Laidlaw to his friend's astonishment. "I am not a bachelor from choice, Morse. I am as human as you are."

"I'm afraid that you met the wrong woman once," thought Morse, but he did not speak his thoughts. Instead, he asked: "Did you notice that the lake water is noticeably warm?"

"The priests mentioned it," Laidlaw replied. "They say it is a recurrent phenomena that precedes activity in the volcano, and they are rather glad of it. I imagine it gives them an opportunity to renew their grip on the credulity of the people by ceremonials. They can magnify their own importance and supposedly ward off the calamity by appeasing the wrath of the gods."

CHAPTER VIII
AULUS THE GLADIATOR

The games were held in an amphitheater hewn from living rock on a volcanic islet not far from the mainland. Laidlaw was quickly ushered off into a group of priests, and Morse found that he was to share a seat in the royal lodge between the two monarchs.

Rana claimed his attentions immediately.

Morse looked to Kiron who merely shrugged and smiled. But when the opportunity afforded itself, he whispered: "Beware of the Flower of Everlasting Sleep. Do not inhale the fragrance. It intoxicates, but it is fatal."

The Atlantean games opened with a procession of maidens, singing and bearing great armfuls of flowers with which they strewed the arena. Trumpeters with long-necked instruments circled the arena, accompanied by a band of priests. They halted at the royal lodge and hailed its occupants by name. Morse was surprised to hear himself included.

A second halt was made on the opposite side of the arena before a purple canopy. Morse was able to make out the figure of Ru — and beside him Laidlaw — as the hailing ceremony was repeated.

A strange perfume arose from the crushed petals that filled the arena. The air was clear, and the rays of the sun were warm and dazzling for the mid-afternoon spectacle. Morse fought to stay clear of Rana's intense being and a repetition of their first meeting. He concentrated on the arena, asked questions profusely, and finally with a slight smile Kiron came to his aid — to the obvious displeasure of his co-ruler.

The monarch spoke of many things: of traditions and ancient festivals, of horses — unknown in New Atlantis and known only through the lore of the past — of cattle. Kiron revealed that they possessed cattle, but their herd had shrunk and bulls were a scarcity. They were used only upon very special occasions — "of which this is one," he added diplomatically.

A quartet of footraces began the arena activities, and when they had been completed wreaths of gilded leaves were bestowed upon the victors by the monarchs. Immediately following, a bull made its appearance. It was a magnificent creature, white, spotted with black, with gilded horns and hoofs, and a garland of roses about its neck. The crowd acclaimed it, calling it by name as if it were some stage favorite.

To those who were thirsty for blood-letting, this was a disappointment. Bulls were too scarce to be killed and served merely as a motive for an exhibition of marvelous agility. Youths and maidens armed with long spears and shorter darts attacked the brute, but the points of their weapons were short, and hardly drew blood. The bull was driven into a frenzy and finally into a sullen fit. A girl vaulted lightly to its neck, seized its horns, and rode off in triumph as her companions prodded the creature to an exit.

The gladiatorial games that followed provided the cue for general excitement. The weapons were real and the men in earnest. They fought in bands at first, then in couples: a javelin thrower, clad only in a linen breechcloth, protected by a partner with broad-bladed sword and a shield almost as long as himself. So dexterous were they that few serious wounds were dealt in the minutes allowed to each bout by the arena master. Still, there was blood enough to bring fierce shouts from their adherents on the benches.

Morse turned away from the action. He saw the beautiful mouth of Rana take on lines, saw her eyes glaze with crimson like some fierce beast. There was no hypnosis here. Morse knew Rana now; knew she could never hold him in trance again. He turned to Kiron who watched somewhat wearily, while making expert comments on the moves of the battlers.

The finest gladiators had been reserved for single combat, and the crowd shouted for its favorites. Occasionally, a winner, still breathing heavily, would advance to a spot before a group of nobles and offer a challenge to the amateurs. There would be a pause, and finally a young aristocrat would rise, cast away his outer garments amidst the cheers of the spectators, and descend to the arena. At times, the professionals were hard pressed, but for the most part they treated their opponents with a good-humored tolerance born of conscious superiority.

Last of all came the boxers, deep-chested giants of heavier mold — men who flailed at each other within the limits of a square indicated by upright posts. Their hands were protected with leather bands bound about the knuckles, fastened at the wrists, and studded with bronze. Two slaves fought ferociously for a prize of freedom, one felling the other with a savage blow upon the temple, and watching with a grin as the loser was dragged away, dying and insensible.

The Atlanteans fought stripped save for the cestus on the knuckles, and adhered to rules that precluded wrestling and kicking. The fights ended with one combatant owning himself beaten or unable to continue. The winners that came for their victory wreaths were badly bruised, but apparently they were Rana's favorites for she added to their wreaths gold coins from a bag brought by an attendant.

Few of the boxers challenged the spectators, and there were no takers, a fact which brought jeers of derision from the populace. Apparently they were not keen to face a possible disfigurement or bad beating.

The final bout ended with a victory for the champion of Atlantis. He was a massive man, weighing well over two hundred and fifty pounds, his powerful body a mass of gnarled muscles and brute strength. The sympathy of the spectators was with his opponent, a lighter, younger man who circled about his foe, raining upon him a torrent of quick swinging blows. The champion waited patiently, dodging and guarding some of the blows, but taking many full upon his features. Finally, the lighter man slowed his attack, breathing heavily from his exertions. And this seemed to be a signal for the champion's strategy. He leaped forward with ponderous arms swinging, too suddenly for his tired opponent to dodge completely away. A glancing blow slowed him, and then one great blow from the champion caught the challenger full on the base of the skull. The latter crumpled without a sound.

The victor advanced with a lurching swagger toward the royal box. His bestial features, scarred in earlier fights, were livid and bruised where the blows of his most recent opponent had gone home. Tiny, piglike eyes glared at Morse from beneath scarred brows. A trickle of blood dripped from his nose, but the broad chest of the fighter rose and fell evenly — as if he had not even exerted himself.

"So, Aulus, you are still champion," said Rana as she bent to place the wreath upon the low brow and dropped some clinking coins into the cestus-bound palm. "This is but a tithe I won on you from the king today."

"I have always contested that Aulus is clumsy," said Kiron, as casually as if he had been discussing the points of a hound. "Some day a quicker, more intelligent man will come along. Diagoras was beaten before he tied on his cestus, beaten by a title."

"Which I still hold," grinned Aulus. "Diagoras will fight no more. I struck the marrow from his spine. Aulus is still champion — unless" — he hesitated for a moment, as if fearful of his own boldness — "unless someone should lift this and take away my wreath."

He stepped back, took off the bloodstained cestus from his left hand, raised it toward Morse, looking straight at him, and flung it to the sand in front of the royal box.

There could be no mistaking the directness of the challenge, nor the taunting leer in the gladiator's eyes. The arena caught the situation as one person and grew silent. Morse felt himself the target of a thousand eyes. Beside him, Rana leaned forward, her lips parted, her eyes bent upon his face. Across the wide arena he could distinguish Laidlaw standing upon his feet.

Kiron touched his arm and whispered to him. With Aulus still glaring at him, the silence was overwhelming. Morse dimly caught some words: " — a trick of Ru." But his blood was mounting under the eyes of the champion. If there were some trick, the only way to circumvent it would be to beat the champion at his own game or lose all prestige for himself and Laidlaw.

He rose, and the spectators lost their silence. They rose with him, cheered, pushed, and the arena became a bedlam. Morse vaulted lightly onto the victor's platform, ran down the steps to where the cestus lay, and held it aloft. The dark eyes of Rana caught his own. They tried to see into them, and a baffled look passed over the beautiful face. Morse knew that she was trying to calculate his chances of victory; she looked for fear, for courage, for stupidity, and looked for other intangibles. And Morse knew that she saw — nothing!

The noise of the arena gradually subsided, and Kiron's modulated voice called: "Thrice the amount of the bet against Aulus once again, Rana."

And Morse was surprised by the answer.

"You tempt me to discourtesy. I wager on our guest."

At these words, the face of Aulus turned into a scowl. He took up the cestus that Morse tossed upon the platform, and looked long into the crowd. Morse had turned without a word and followed the arena master into the gymnasium. Strange butterflies crawled within his stomach for he was not one to seek out a fight. Still, he told himself, the Atlantean boxers were clumsy — punchers. He believed in his own skill, and he had taken lessons from modern experts. Morse hoped that his boxing ability, his speed of hand and foot, and his conditioning would offset the superior weight and brute strength of Aulus.

The American was seized with an intense desire to defeat this swaggerer, and his butterflies disappeared.

In the gymnasium he stripped to a loin cloth and allowed himself to be rubbed with oils by a sad-eyed man who proclaimed himself the trainer of the slain Diagoras. When it came time to don the cestus, there were none save those belonging to the gladiators.

"Give me those of Diagoras," said Morse.

The trainer brought them reluctantly.

"I fear that they are covered with misfortune," he said.

"They are covered with the blood of Aulus," replied Morse grimly. "More of it will wipe away the evil."

"That is well spoken," said the trainer, and then in an aside: "Beware of his right arm. And if he appears to weaken in any way, then be most wary."

Morse nodded understanding and stepped into the arena, knowing now that civilization was far behind. A throaty roar greeted him as he crossed the sand. Flowers flung by half the populace littered his path, as many tried to emulate their rulers by making him their favorite. But many were quiet, and Morse knew that they had wagered on the professional.

As he advanced Morse felt a strange sense of exultation as if some ancestor — or he himself in a former incarnation — had once trod the arena to pit his strength and skill against another's.

Aulus waited disdainfully, leaning his bulk against one of the pillars of the fight space. When his opponent was only a few paces away, he coiled suddenly like some great reptile ready to strike. Morse waited expectantly, but the arena master hurried between them, and with a few words led the two before the royal box. Right arms extended, they hailed the monarchs.

Rana gazed at them in anticipation of the savage sport that was to follow. The fire of her eyes held those of Aulus, but Morse turned his glance to Kiron's face. The monarch's lips moved silently and quickly, and the American read the words: "right lower ribs."

Accompanied by the arena master, the combatants moved in a measured step to the square that was to be their place of conflict.-The two were of a height, but the shoulders of Aulus were broader, and his chest and hips formed a square torso, in distinction to that of Morse, whose frame sloped inward to narrow hips. The American's muscles were long and less visible than those of the professional; and his legs, though well-developed, were saplings beside the huge boughs of the gladiator.

Morse's trip through the jungle had left him in fine condition, without an extra ounce of weight. Aulus was a trifle gross with good living, although his wind had seemed excellent in the earlier combat. Morse remembered the wild swings of the Atlantean boxers and planed to treat the populace to an exhibition of jolting straight arm punches. He hoped they would be a disconcerting surprise to Aulus, who owned a sixty pound weight advantage. "Jabbing and footwork," he told himself.

The combatants took their places, and after a look to Kiron, the arena master dropped his baton, the signal that commenced the battle.

Distaining his opponent for a moment, Aulus carefully placed his right foot forward, the left hand on guard, and the right hand opposite his breast in the now familiar Atlantean form. Morse opposed him loosely, hands high, poised on both feet ready to move in and out with lightning thrusts.

The arena had fallen silent again, and the battlers could hear the chirp of a bird from an outer tier. Aulus stood like a rock, derisively smiling with swollen lips that disclosed teeth broken from cestus blows. Morse felt a fury to erase the mocking grimace. He advanced, feinted with his left, drawing up the right hand of Aulus. Instantly Morse led with his right hand, and followed with a low smash to the ribs, side-stepping the wild counter swings.

Aulus grunted as the blow smashed home, and Morse knew that at some time his man had been injured sufficiently for him to favor a spot that might hold a weakness. The cruel cestus studs had ripped the skin, and blood ran down the gladiator's flanks, bringing a shout from the benches. Raging, Aulus wheeled and charged with a flurry of blows. So swift and determined was the attack that Morse had barely time to deliver a straight left hand to the face before he was forced to cover and retreat. The hammering of the great arms, hard as bronze, threatened to smash down his defense.

Feeling left his forearms. And while a clinch would have given him a breather, grappling was forbidden in the arena. A roar told him that he had retreated beyond the limits of the square, and he side-stepped nimbly to gain the center. Aulus floundered after him, and Morse saw that he had opened up a flowing wound above the eye and on the cheek bone. The Atlantean dashed the blood aside and charged with a thunderous growl, only to run into another straight jab. Morse ducked under a wild swing, and as the gladiator pivoted off balance he was pounded heavily below the heart.

Aulus' left eye was closing fast. He bellowed his rage at this agile opponent who fought in so unorthodox a manner. Morse danced in and out with quick, sharp blows, but he did not go untouched. Once a glancing swing had all but paralyzed his shoulder and left arm, and on another occasion the cestus had cut his cheek. He felt the blood dripping down as he countered to the lower ribs and once again got a responsive grunt of pain. Morse's arms ached from blocking punches, but Aulus' face was now a gory mask. And yet there was no weakening to the Atlantean's blows.

Aulus now stood in the center of the square, revolving like some clumsy turret as Morse moved around him. His unclosed eye glowered red with a venomous determination, and as Morse planted an uppercut squarely on his jaw, the gladiator shook off the blow with a laugh. The man appeared as invincible as an oak.

The sound from the benches seemed far away, as breaking waves on a distant beach, and the American found himself longing for Queensbury rules and the attention of deft seconds during a breathing spell.

With a third blow to the ribs Aulus staggered back, mouth open, face distorted, arms lowered. Morse leaped forward to press his attack. And suddenly the gladiator. regained his full strength, his features demoniac with anticipated triumph. Morse knew that he had been lured into the trap against which he had been warned. A smashing blow stung him sideways, and before he could regain his balance another pushed past his guard and caught him over the heart. His lungs failed; the air grew dark; he reeled dizzily. Only the absolute condition of his legs kept him on his feet as he crouched instinctively. Thunder sounded in his ears, and he felt that the end had come.

But no blows fell. The mist cleared away, and he looked out from under his guard. Aulus was on the ground. The force of the misjudged blow he had meant to end the combat had brought him crashing to the sand. Morse summoned all his reserve and sprang at him like a tiger. The gladiator was rising from his left knee, his right arm extended upward. There was a livid bruise on the ribs where Morse had made his target, and as Aulus straightened to full height the American punched with all his force to this spot. Aulus groaned and dropped his hands. The blow had cracked his ribs, sending the splintered bone inward. Morse's right hand went home to the jaw, his left to the Adam's apple.

The giant tottered. His knees sagged and he confusedly raised one arm to clear the blood from his eyes, now both blinded. Instinctively he tried to protect his head. Morse shifted all his weight to his left foot, and put every ounce of power into a final punch. It caught Aulus between the parting of the ribs, battering the force of its impact through the muscles of the diaphragm.

Morse caught the look of unfeigned agony on the chopped countenance and stepped back. The mighty bulk wavered, the coordination between brain and nerve and muscle failed, and he crashed to the ground, a palpitating mass.

Morse stood aside as the arena master hurried up. The air was rent with salvos of applause and cries of consternation and disbelief. The official beckoned to the American. Aulus was writhing in pain as Morse bent over him.

"It is enough!" he cried. "I am undone. Beaten and blind. Bear me away, Milo. I yield my wreath."

CHAPTER IX
THE INITIATION

Morse was the new idol of the populace. Whenever he appeared, crowds made way for him with cries of admiration; while the maidens, who perpetually wore wreaths of heavy-scented blossoms, cast them before him so that his existence out of doors was almost a continued triumphal procession. And since the games, Rana had increased her attentions. She showered him with gifts and invitations, and all but openly declared herself willing to accept him as lover and husband.

Morse could admire her from a distance for she was unquestionably a beautiful woman. But his fascination for her was gone; she held no spell for him now. And he avoided her as much as possible. Finally, as the month drew to its close, he spoke to Laidlaw.

"Look," he said. "I can't take much more of this. I have to work at avoiding her. How soon are you going to be ready to leave?"

Laidlaw looked at him in bewildered surprise. "Leave! I haven't even begun my work here. Next week is the start of the month of Pasiphae; the month of Demeter follows. I must observe the festivals and their ritual. They may be close to those of three thousand years ago. This is an expedition into the past; you can't be serious about leaving at this time. I have six months' work in front of me — a year's."

So enamored was Laidlaw of his subject that he forgot Morse's appeal. "The only thing that bothers me is the lack of film for the camera. We should have brought a motion picture outfit, Morse. Think of it — tangible proof, the scientific value. Why didn't we bring one?"

"I don't want to interrupt your researches," said Morse in a tone that secured the scientist's wandering attention, "but we may have to get away from here in a hurry. You know what Rana's attitude is. I don't think I can be diplomatic toward her much longer without insulting her. Our affairs are going to come to a crisis some day soon, and when I break with her there's going to be trouble.

"I dodged her last week by staying across the lake, and at that she sent me a letter each day and a jewel which she claims is a vital part of my costume. Rana is as clever as she is beautiful, Laidlaw. Ambitious, too, but she holds nothing for me. She spins a web of circumstance that puts us together, and she may want to make me her consort. But somewhere along the line she's going to try and do away with Kiron, and if this happens Ru is going to be right there. He's either going to control her, or failing that he's going to eliminate her just as she intends to eliminate Kiron."

Laidlaw nodded gravely, his work forgotten for the moment.

"You may be right. If Ru can himself while we're still here, we're going to find ourselves out on the ledge with the vultures some morning, and there won't be any rescue party."

The scientist went on slowly. "I've often wondered how genuine her interest in you really is. In the beginning I thought it was feigned — completely so; that she and Ru were working hand in hand against Kiron and against us as well. Now, I'm not so sure about Rana. You're too strong of mind for her, and you baffle her. She's still power-hungry beyond belief, but she can't conquer you and I believe that this fascinates her.

"You know Kiron has been anxious to honor us by giving us the full citizenship he promised when we rescued him. Now, I think Rana has come over to this idea as well, while Ru has been quietly working against it all along. You see, if they initiate us to the level of nobles as Kiron intends, it would afford us a little more protection against anything that the old priest might have planned for us. Anyway, I think we have some sort of a conflict growing between Rana and Ru, and you may very well be the cause of it."

"Laidlaw, if you can see that much, you can see the problems facing us if we stay here."

Laidlaw nodded his head sadly. "You're right, of course. But I've got to have a month for my work. Somehow, you've got to smooth things over for that long. Morse, I implore you. . ."

Morse had to laugh at the other's seriousness. "All right, then. One month. It's not going to be easy. And don't say anything about our intention to depart. We'll have to fly at the last moment — with Kiron's aid if we can get it."

As the days passed, Rana took up the cause to ennoble Morse and Laidlaw. Since the former had defeated Aulus in the arena, her interest was — as Laidlaw sensed — more genuine. And when she finally, in a public speech, championed the honor due the visitors, Ru's powerful opposition fell silently away with the applause of the populace.

Morse was to receive the second degree of epoptae, and Laidlaw, by reason of his dwarfed and misshapen legs, was to receive the slightly lesser degree of mystae. (Morse wondered how much was due to his companion's imperfections and how much was due to Rana's interest in him.)

The initiation took place in the underground chambers of the Temple of the Double Ax, dedicated to the sun and moon gods, Minos and Pasiphae. It was midnight on the last day of the month of Minos when Morse and Laidlaw, clad in ceremonial robes, blindfolded, their ears muffled by a light bandage, another across their mouth and nostrils, were escorted by winding ways to the council chamber. Thirty silent forms wearing long-sleeved robes of gray that fell over their feet were grouped about a central figure occupying a throne carved from the rock wall. Oil lamps cast a flickering light upon the mute assembly. The silent figures all wore masks representing jaguars, human skulls, and the heads of great beaked birds.

The man on the throne was distinguished by a headgear representing a bull. Frescoes dimly showed upon the walls. In the semicircle formed by the initiates stood a glowing brazier supported upon upreared and intertwisting snakes. Incense rose from the green flames of a burning liquid. Morse and Laidlaw were led to a point directly behind it.

"Neophytes!" The voice, despite its resonance, had a strident quality that assured the Americans that Ru was speaking through a megaphone-like object in his mask. "You have been instructed in your behavior. Courage conquers all things. Fear breeds. weakness. This is the wedding night of Minos, son of Zeus, and god of the sun, and Pasiphae, the all-shining, goddess of the moon, deities of the double ax, founders of Atlantis."

As he spoke the altar flame changed first to orange, then to a vivid blue at the mention of the honored names.

"May you be found worthy in their sight to become as their children. Your sight — " (the bandages were removed from their eyes) " —your hearing and your speech — " (the other mufflings followed) " — have been taken from you to be restored as the trials shall prove you fit. Through darkness, danger, and through death the way shall lead back to light and life. Do not step from the trail or those who lurk close by will seize and destroy you."

The light in the brazier died down as the words ceased, flickering to a creeping silver flame that suddenly leaped up and vanished, leaving the chamber in stygian darkness. By its last lambent effort the Americans could see that the chamber had emptied itself of other occupants in some mysterious fashion. The frescoes wavered on the solid walls as if they shook with the passing of the initiates. They caught a glimpse of the vacant throne before blackness enveloped them.

A liquid substance began to drip — spat, spat — upon the pavement with a regularity that timed their pulses to its beat. The darkness thickened; the air grew oppressive with a salty tang — half scent, half flavor; the subtle essence of newly-spilled blood. There were whisperings about them, inarticulate chuckles, grotesque cacklings, and cold blasts of wind passed over them with the beat of invisible wings.

Suddenly eyes appeared in the darkness. They glowed weirdly, green and crimson, moved about them at various heights, and finally settled in two immovable rows, baleful and hypnotic. More ghoulish chuckling and laughter, and the eyes began to whirl. Finally, with an animal chorus of gnashing of teeth, scraping of claws, and fearful howls, silence came to the chamber.

"If we could work anything like that in the States," whispered Morse in English, "we'd have the Psychological Research Society at our feet."

"They've been working at it for thousands of years," replied Laidlaw. "Damned effective."

The dark slowly became less intense, the air laden with the delicate fragrance of spring blossoms. Black turned into purple, and purple became gray, and finally they could see the walls in front of them dissolving in whirls of mist.

Upon a couch lay the exquisite form of a sleeping woman, rounded breasts lifting with her gentle breathing, skin rosy with youth and health. As they gazed, a subtle change occurred. The curves lost their roundness, the flesh shriveled and became blue, the air grew rank with the smell of death.

Before their eyes the infinitely fair creature was falling away, disintegrating. The face became a skull as the flesh withered. The hair, bleached white, fell out in huge chunks; ribs and pelvis bones stood out in horrible distinction; the chamber reeked with the stench of a house. The bones fell away and crumbled, leaving only a little pile of dust from which a snake writhed away.

The wall resumed shape behind the gray veil, and a dazzling light enveloped them. From its center a voice sounded:

"The Eye of Minos witnesses and approves. Behind them another took up the ritual:

"It is recorded. Turn and enter."

A narrow opening appeared to their vision. They crossed the threshold and a door clanged violently behind them. The room was filled with a tremulous blue radiance. At the farther end stood a statue of a woman wearing a helmet crested with the new moon. Hands were raised above its finely carved head, a twisted snake in each. About the statue's body was entwined the scaly coils of an enormous serpent, with its head resting upon the shoulder. Dull eyes gleamed like uncut emeralds. A sound of chanting came from beyond the walls:

> "To thee, All-Shining One Goddess divine!
> Unto thy votaries Vouchsafe a sign.
> Let thy snakes twining Show us thou livest,
> Show us that Pasiphae Still mercy givest Shine on thy votaries Goddess benign."

"Serpents?" said Morse, a question in his voice.

"Pasiphae in her chthonian representation as 'Goddess of the Underworld,'" came the reply.

The light brightened with a brilliance that came in waves like the rays of the aurora borealis. In its shimmer the carven snakes seemed to quiver and the eyes of the great serpent grew brighter.

"Look out, Laidlaw!" cried Morse suddenly. "The brute's alive!"

The head of the ophidian raised from the shoulder of the statue and disappeared, to glide out from beneath the arm in a swift undulation, its jaws open, its tongue vibrating. A whisper of movement was heard as scales scraped over pavement.

The blood of the initiates ran cold as they waited for the reptile's attack. The obscene slithering was the only sound to be heard in the chamber, and they could only guess at its position.

"Ru!" snarled Morse.

Laidlaw kept silent. He had thought from the first glance that the snake was alive, but he believed it had been coiled about the statue in a sluggish state of coma. There was no question of its identity. More than thirty feet in length, it was the most powerful and ill-tempered of all the big serpents, the anaconda.

Suddenly Morse felt a coil encircle his lower leg in a lightning loop and mount to the thigh, compressing it until it seemed that the bone must break. He set his hands on the writhing, clammy body, trying to reach the head, but encountered only a continually thickening coil. He let out an exclamation and it was echoed by Laidlaw. The anaconda had attacked both Americans at the same time, using Morse as a support on which to base the leverage of its constriction.

The firm, unyielding body of the snake offered no hold. The coil about Morse's waist was as thick as his thigh, hard as a hempen cable, resistless, inexorable. His case was desperate, and both men were without weapons. A choking cry came from Laidlaw as Morse strove again to loosen the deadly twist that was slowly squeezing his leg into jelly, at the same time holding him powerless from moving.

"Laidlaw!" he cried.

The choking sound changed to a great sob of relief.

"Ah!" sounded Laidlaw, strength emanating from his voice. "I've got him! He had me about the waist. Now then!"

The long length of the snake whipped into wild action. Morse was thrown violently to the ground, and he felt Laidlaw close beside him. Between them, the infuriated reptile writhed and thrashed, dragging them over the hard stone floor. Laidlaw's breath came in great gasps as he exerted all his strength. Morse felt the coil about his thigh relax, and dragged at it until he freed himself. He tried to rise, but his leg refused to carry his weight. He half crawled toward Laidlaw.

"How can I help you?" he cried.

A grunt answered him. The snake's body lay across that of his friend, writhing more and more feebly. Laidlaw rolled over on top of it.

"I've choked the hellish thing," he gasped. "I think it's dead, but I don't dare let go of it."

A series of dull thuds came to their ears from outside the chamber. The chanting was taken up again:

> "Hear us, O Shining One Grant our desire.
>   Pasiphae! Pasiphae!
>   Dread we thy ire One to the other O Bountiful Mother
>   Accept the gifts we bring As at thy feet we cling,
>   Pasiphae! Pasiphae!
>   All-Shining One."

"I think we were intended to be the gifts," said Laidlaw. "That could well have been our funeral ode."

The flickering radiance was gradually returning, and Morse, now with his own weight on the lower half of the anaconda, saw Laidlaw battering its head, already a shapeless bloody stump, against the stone floor. One loose coil was about his middle, and Morse tugged until it came limply away. The two sat up and looked at each other as Laidlaw flung away the battered head, and Morse kicked at the convulsively twitching mass with his sound leg while he tried to rub the other back to sensibility.

"Cheerful little trick," he said angrily. "The snake of the goddess resenting the intrusion of strangers. That would have been the verdict, I suppose. Ru full of regrets and the snake full of us. Ugh! How did you manage to get hold of its neck?"

"Good luck! The devil has ruined my digestion forever, though."

Morse started to laugh, and Laidlaw found himself echoing him. In the reaction to their danger, they laughed half-hysterically until they could force themselves to their feet. The scientist rubbed his stomach. My is jellied. How's your leg?"

Morse prodded it and winced. "It's sound, but it's sore as the devil."

"Well, if Ru planned this," said Laidlaw, "he did a good job. He had an alibi ready."

The mystic voice broke into the chamber:

"Advance, O neophytes!"

A section of the wall slid downward and they passed through the opening into natural light, leaving the dying snake behind. At a junction of the low corridor, a gray and shapeless figure with a skull mask stood beckoning to them. Had this proved to be Ru, Morse felt that he could have done away with him then and there. But the voice of this sentinel quickly betrayed the presence as Kiron.

"The mystae to the right," he said, "your test has ended. Yours, epoptae, to the left," adding in a lower tone: "And courage, brother, even in darkness."

Laidlaw held back a moment, but Morse urged him on.

"If they plan to do us harm we can't escape it," he said, and took the left-hand passage. It ended almost before it had begun in another gloomy chamber that grew totally dark when the door closed behind his entrance. A voice like that of a ventriloquist, its source indeterminate, accosted him.

"Now comes the final choice, epoptae. Perhaps it lies with you. Who knows? Perhaps the gods direct. Yet it is on your action that the issue hangs. Gaze and ponder before your body answers to your settled will."

With a clang, a door slid back, and a gush of heat surged into the room. A fire glared in a passage beyond the door, pulsing with swift plays of molten orange and vermilion. The portal closed, and a second door revealed four leaping, maneless cat-creatures. Large as full-grown lions, they were skin-clad in ebony velvet, with topaz eyes, crimson mouths, and sabered ivory fangs. The beasts sprang at him and roared in frenzy as a barred gate rose up before them.

A third exit lifted, and a breath of night air, mingled with flower perfume and the clean smell of the lake, stole into his nostrils. The way lay open up a slight incline to a point where silver moonlight bathed an open causeway. As this was shut out, the voice came to him:

"Commend the prompting of your will unto the gods. As they judge you, so shall you go scatheless or to your doom."

The floor beneath him started to revolve slowly, not enough to disturb his balance, but acquiring speed enough to wipe out any lingering idea he might hold of the location of the respective doors.

Morse had entered the ordeal in the belief that the initiation was calculated to break the nerves of a superstitious man. The fight with the snake had disturbed his confidence; but his wrath, somewhat calmed by Kiron's friendly message, was still dominant enough to wish to put a swift end to what he still believed to be a combination of masquerade and optical illusion.

Without hesitation, he moved to the wall. One hand encountered a projection; the other, sliding over the vertical surface, passed from coolness to heat, slight but distinctly noticeable. He moved along the contour of the chamber until he felt a second knob, and bent, listening intently. Did he hear the faint sound of muffled growls? Morse wondered if the tests might hold real quality.

Swiftly he sought the third latch, found it, clutched and pulled. It resisted, but then slid readily before a side thrust. Before him rose the incline to the moonlit causeway, and pure air met him as he ran up the rise.

Gulping the sweet air into his lungs, he reached the causeway. Behind him the egress had closed, and the carven facade of the temple showed in gray and purple silence. Morse crossed the causeway to a balustrade and leaned upon it. The crescent moon faintly outlined the temple on the isle of Sele. Here was the realm of Leola, sister of Rana, and her Dianae.

A breeze blew off the lake, and suddenly Morse wondered if this beautiful Leola could hold any of the magical enchantment that her island did, there in the moonlight. Below him, a galley with oars supplementing a silvered sail reached silently for a wharf. He straightened from his thoughts, his arms folded on the wide baluster rail, then turned reluctantly to move away. A soft, thudding rush of feet sounded behind him. A cloth was thrown over his head, and the gathered folds pinned his arms to his sides.

Morse fought against the arms that sought to hold him and lift him from his feet. Coarse oaths came to his ears, sounding dimly through the muffling linen. Then, still struggling, he was lifted from his feet and borne away.

A voice rang out. It was high pitched and as sweetly clear as the sound of a silver trumpet. His captors paused and set him down.

"Who are you who dare to profane the bridal night of Pasiphae? Stand, before I turn you into stone!"

Morse heard the mumbling apologies of the men who had attacked him. The cloth was hastily removed, and he faced his rescuer.

It was a woman. She was slender and tall, clothed in garments that glittered, one arm raised . There was something strangely familiar about her face. It was clean-carven, imperious, set like a flower upon a neck that was as round and smooth as a column. Hair, piled high, glinted pale gold in the moonlight. Two eyes burned like azure stars.

The woman stood on the causeway. Behind her were a score of her fair sex, clad in white garments with ornaments that gleamed as they moved.

"Who are you?" she asked. "And why does this rabble molest you?"

The men who had seized him slunk away as Morse answered.

"I am one of the strangers to Atlantis." And as he spoke he knew that this was Leola. Her likeness to Rana could not be mistaken. But here was a refinement of feature, a majesty that the queen could not approach.

"I have no idea who these are who have attacked me," he continued, "though I might make a guess. The night has not been altogether fortunate for me — until now."

She surveyed him with a disdain that was tempered by a half-concealed curiosity.

"You are the one who conquered Aulus," she said, "and tonight you became an epoptae. Are you so enamored of Atlantis that you would forsake your own land?"

"I have never been enamored — until this moment," he answered truthfully, his eyes upon hers. Did her eyes waver?

"Your words are idle," she said.

"Yet I would thank you for my rescue."

"I would not willingly see even a man harmed," came the reply.

"Even a man!" Morse repeated the words out loud and smiled. "Still I thank you. And I thank the gods, Leola, that I am a man — and that you are a woman." Again her eyes seemed to waver.

"I do not read the meaning of your words," she said, and some of her assurance was gone.

"They are not hard to understand," he answered. "But the key lies not in the mind, but in the heart."

A knot of men was hurrying toward them, and a voice called his name. It was Laidlaw.

"Here are my friends," said Morse. "Again I thank you, Leola. We will meet again."

She made no answer save for an uptilt of that haughty head, and stepped backward, still facing him, until her women surrounded her. Only then did Morse turn to greet his friends.

"Le-o-la!" he said, just above his breath, testing the liquid syllables. "Le-o-la! The name fits her. It is like the murmur of moonlit ripples upon a silver beach."

CHAPTER X
THE ISLE OF SELE

Kiron came in upon the two Americans the next morning shortly after their plunge. Four automatic pistols and belts lay upon the low couch, and he picked up one of them.

"You expect trouble?" he asked seriously.

"We are going to start it, Kiron," answered Morse — "start it at the first hint that the other fellow is even thinking about it."

He buckled the belt about his waist. "After this, Laidlaw and I are going to feel a lot safer with these handy, and I'd appreciate it if you would send Maya and Xolo to us for some additional support. I've had enough of this sort of thing."

He exposed his leg, deep purple and yellow where the anaconda had crushed it.

"My middle's in the same shape," said Laidlaw. "Hereafter I've got a special grudge against snakes, including a certain two-legged one."

Kiron looked puzzled, and Morse related what had happened in the shrine of Pasiphae and the attempt to capture him afterward.

"There is no snake about the middle of the statue," said the king. "It must have been placed there to destroy you."

He mused thoughtfully. "Ru might have said that the snake appeared to resist the profanation of the shrine by strangers. But since you passed the ordeal successfully, you have some measure of protection. I don't think you will be attacked on the street, though I will send your Indians to you.

"There are strange things working in Atlantis. Unseen politics, disaffection among the soldiers. With no outer enemies to fear, our military is recruited for police duty, though every noble keeps up the practice of arms. Ru and the priests control a force of Indians who have been well trained. It is plain they constitute a menace. There has been grumbling over taxes, which are light enough, and a disposition to break through old rules regarding nobility; almost all the elements of rebellion are slowly fermenting.

"But these are not your troubles," he added. "I should not burden you with them. I came to ask you to breakfast with me."

"My stomach is in sad condition," grinned Laidlaw, "but this is a good chance to test it. And one should never discuss politics on an empty stomach."

As they ate, Kiron outlined the festivities of the month of Pasiphae. It was the month of planting, the wedding of seeds with the earth — an occasion in which the priestesses of the moon goddess took a prominent part. Many gifts were thrown into the lake to propitiate the god that dwelt beneath the water, and these Kiron expected to be unusually valuable and numerous owing to the gradually increasing warmth of the water. The festivals would end with a joint service in worship of the double-ax deities.

"Not too many years ago the priests used to sacrifice maidens to Minos," said Kiron, "and youths to Pasiphae. But this custom is no longer practiced, for which I am thankful. Ru resents this loss and loses no opportunity to prophesy trouble in consequence. But the people are tired of innocent blood being spilled.

"By the way, Morse," asked Kiron, "did Leola speak to you?"

Morse felt his face grow hot. Even as Kiron had been speaking, his mind had been wandering to thoughts of this priestess. He had dreamt of her through the night, and he pondered a little that she had so filled his thoughts. At the same moment Kiron had questioned him, Morse was wondering if he had fallen in love.

"Yes," he answered, still embarrassed. "She did speak to me. As a matter of fact she referred to me as 'even a man,' as if she was issuing an order to her followers not to tread on worms."

"That's the way she feels about us," laughed Kiron. "I have a grudge against her myself. She won over the girl who was learning to return my love. Now she is Leola's first priestess."

"Who is she?" asked Laidlaw.

"Lycida," returned the king. "A beautiful creature, . and far more human than Leola. We'll see a good deal of both of them in the next day or so. If I were you," — he looked warningly at Morse — "I wouldn't let Rana catch you looking in the direction of her younger sister. She's loved her a lot more since Leola took her stand against men and went off to Sele."

Rana welcomed Morse to the stand erected for the royal court upon the palace steps. She did not even acknowledge Laidlaw. Morse managed to conceal his limp, not caring to discuss its origin with her in front of Ru, who inquired after his health with a placid assurance of friendship.

"After the festival," whispered Rana — she had a trick of making the most trivial utterances sound confidential — "I have planned an entertainment at my villa at the southern end of the lake. Cnidus, the poet, has written a drama — 'The End of Eros,' he calls it — that is a satire on our affairs. And we are all going to take part in it. You and Kiron may go hunting the cave beast while we rehearse if you promise not to get hurt."

She leaned toward him languorously, her breath upon his cheek, her bare arm, soft as satin, lightly touching the length of his. Morse felt unusually irritant. His leg throbbed, and he had much the same feeling that a bird has when its feet first stick to a lined twig. He answered shortly, and Rana drew back, half-offended.

"You are ill-tempered this morning," she said. "One would think you were your friend over there. Look at that sulky brute!"

Morse could not retain his smile as he glanced at Laidlaw, who was not in the least sulky.

"That's better," breathed Rana; "I had almost begun to hate you." She shot him a glance that held more than a hint of temper. Morse remembered his promise to Laidlaw and spurred himself to lighter talk, wondering in the meantime how he could escape the threatened visit to the villa.

The morning was magnificent. At the far end of the lake, twenty-five miles away, the crater was outlined in sharp relief. The water was a deep sapphire. Here and there boats carrying large numbers of spectators came on under sail and oar, straddling like giant water bugs. A ceremonial barge from Sele was midway to the shore, and the sweet voices of the priestesses came faintly to them. The causeway that bordered the lake was strewn ankle deep with flowers, and water bearers passed along refreshing them so that they might render their full fragrance as they were crushed beneath the feet of the procession.

A blare of trumpets came from the temple steps, and a company of priests in gleaming golden robes made their way to the landing to greet the priestesses of Pasiphae. Ru, after making his courtesies, had disappeared from the royal box.

The route was lined with spectators of all ages, and shifting colors from their bright-hued garments gave the effect of a flower garden in a breeze. Behind the palace the volcano cast its morning shadow across that quarter of Atlantis, and a fume of vapor issued from its snow cap in irregular puffs.

Silence fell as the spectators craned their necks. A long fanfare of trumpets ended, and the sound of chanting became more and more pronounced. The procession had started.

First to appear were a company of children, some of whom sang in shrill, sweet voices. Others played a simple tune upon a double pipe. Older youths and maidens followed, leading with garlands a snow-white bull with gilded horns and hoofs, a wreath about its massive neck — all that remained of the grisly minotaur worship once found in ancient Crete.

The priest's guard was headed by a giant Indian, of that strange race who were long servitors to the Atlanteans. Clad in jaguar skins, a crested helmet, and with a chain of gold upon his great chest, he glanced insolently about him. Forewarned by Kiron's talk at breakfast, Morse detected an arrogance, a swagger, dominating the entire bodyguard, and he believed that rebellion was contained here only by the prospect of license to come.

Ru rode in their center in an open litter, his head shaded by a heavily fringed canopy held by four slaves. Behind him marched a column of priests, carrying for a standard the emblem of the double ax. More of the Indian bodyguard appeared, with sullen jaguars held in check by short bronze chains. The front ranks of the spectators shrank back until a body of gladiators paraded before them. Among them was Aulus, who cast a malevolent glare at Morse as he passed.

Athletes of both sexes walked with the bulls of the arena. A break in the procession was closed by maidens strewing white-petaled, fresh flowers, and others carrying wicker cages from which they released white doves, emblems of Pasiphae. The Americans had an unpleasant reminder as a dozen girls marched by with serpents twining about their arms and throats and white bodies. But these snakes were boars, none over ten feet in length, and mild-dispositioned pets of the temple.

A hundred priestesses, dark hair bound with fillets of silver to uphold a crescent-moon disk, sleeveless garments shot with the same metal, swung by disdainfully, chanting as they went. Morse barely noticed them, waiting for the approach of the high priestess. He sat erect, his face alight, his eagerness unconcealed. Rana leaned back, watching him intently, as if suddenly suspicious of his interest. Kiron, too, was now alert, shaken from the usual pose which he wore in public.

She came at last, abreast with two other litters of ivory on which her lieutenants reclined. Above them were silken awnings of azure, studded with silver stars. A single priestess dared a swift, shy glance at the court, then turned away as Kiron stirred in his seat.

Leola lay indifferent to the crowd, her face as serene as the full moon, the exquisite outline of her form revealed by her clinging drapery. One bare, rounded arm lay so that the taper fingers drooped over the edge of the litter, one arched, silver-sandaled foot peeping from the brocaded hem of her robe.

There was confusion among the gladiators. Two of the bulls were out of control, and the procession halted. Irresistibly attracted, Morse gazed at Leola, his heart in his eyes. Slowly under his gaze the high priestess turned her head toward him as golden poppies turn toward the sun. The white lids — he could trace the tiny blue veins upon them — lifted, and her dark eyes looked into his. An invisible bridge was formed. Morse felt his spirit stealing out upon it, and knew that hers had come to meet it. A rosy blush transfused her face, the blush spreading to her neck and flooding the ivory of her arm to the fingertips, like Pygmalion's marble Galatea slowly coming to life under the sculptor's compelling love.

Trumpets sounded and the procession resumed its march. Leola's litter passed. The connection established by their glances snapped as an electric current dies with the turn of a switch, and Morse gave an involuntary sigh that released the breath he had been holding in.

Beside him, he became suddenly conscious of Rana's presence; he turned. The queen's face was sphinxlike, and the spots of rouge she affected stood out against her pallor like crimson bruises. Her eyes were as hard and glittering as those of the anaconda at the shrine.

"So," she spoke slowly, picking her words, "you and. my sister seem attracted by each other! It is strange, indeed, for she has disavowed men both by preference and by oath. She may change one, but do not tempt her to break the other. It would mean death for both of you — unless —"

She stopped speaking, her hands shaking like a wintry leaf, her voice trembling! "You have seen her before?" she almost hissed.

Morse answered her quietly, wondering at his own calmness.

"She rescued me last night when some of your cutthroats set upon me. I suspect I have her to thank for my life."

"Ah!" Rana relaxed, and some of the cruelty left her eyes, though suspicion still lurked in their depths. "Who were these men?"

"They came at me swiftly," he replied, "and later they slunk quietly into the shadows. They were Indians, but not slaves. They wore swords."

Rana's brows met, and she compressed her lips. "They shall be punished," she said aloud; and to herself: "And you, my sister, shall be watched."

The court rose after the procession had passed, making their way, first by litter and then by boats, to a great float roofed with silken curtains. Here they feasted and watched the ceremony of propitiation. Ru and his priests descended the water stairs of the temple, and as the men chanted, cast objects into the water that glittered as they whirled and shot out colored sparks from the gems that incrusted them. Then they ranged themselves on either side, as Leola and her attendants repeated the action. The populace lined the balustrade, waiting for a signal for their share in the sacrifice.

It came with a blast of trumpets, and a shower of ornaments rained into the lake. The trumpets were repeated, and at each blast gold and gems broke the water's surface. Kiron tossed in a miniature replica of the double ax, but Morse noticed that the nobles cast their share not overliberally.

"It is all a great waste," said Rana, as she slipped a magnificent bracelet from her wrist. Still, it satisfies the people and keeps the artificers busy. You, too, must sacrifice, now that you are a noble of Atlantis."

"I have nothing valuable but what you have given me," said Morse. He spoke as a matter of fact, but Rana smiled and laid her hand upon his arm with a lingering pressure.

"That was a courtier's speech," she said. "Give me that fibula."

He took the golden ornament that was strangely like an elaborate safety pin from his mantle and handed it to her. She plucked a silver cord from the fringe of her rainbow-plaided girdle and tied the pin to her bracelet, then turned and tossed the two offerings into the air together. The knot slipped, and the offerings fell apart before they reached the water. There was an involuntary silence among the nobles, and Kiron smiled. Rana shot him a murderous look, her face distorted like that of Medusa.

"Poseidon refuses your combination, cousin," mocked Kiron. "The omens are not favorable."

"I hate you!" she hissed. Kiron only laughed, and Rana bent an inscrutable look upon Morse. There was tragedy here, and apprehension, and a purpose that he could not quite understand.

"The ceremonial is over," she said abruptly. "It is useless to wait longer. Let us return to the palace."

She rose petulantly, summoning the boats, but she did not ask him to join her for the return. With open relief, Morse took a seat beside Laidlaw.

The conclusion of the ritual was a signal for the crowd to depart. This was done in a confusion of oars and sails that produced much laughter and shouting. Somehow, a lane was cleared for the ceremonial barge of the high priestess of Pasiphae, a cumbersome, top-heavy craft with a shrine built high upon its stern. It was towed by ropes from two galleys, rowed by lesser priestesses and neophytes.

A sudden wind blew from the cliffs and sent the cluster of boats into a hopeless entanglement. Laughter was replaced by cries of consternation. Morse saw that the royal float had been torn from its moorings, and, impelled by the strong wind upon its awnings and curtains, it bore down on the overladen boats.

The float was high out of water, and heavily built; it was a formidable engine of destruction as it drove before the fury of this sudden gale. Women and children screamed, and men fought hard to clear their boats from its path. It smashed into an open shallop, driving the craft beneath the water as its occupants were dragged aboard a larger vessel. A second float was destroyed, and the float now threatened the barge of the priestesses.

The oarswomen towing the barge faltered in their stroke, undecided as to a course of action. Morse, recognizing the frail construction of the barge, urged his rowers forward. In the face of imminent danger, Leola remained calm, but below her women huddled together in fear. The heavy float crashed into the stern of the barge, and the shrine, insecurely attached, first rocked and then toppled into the water amid the shrieks of the onlookers.

Leola moved suddenly as the platform tottered, springing to clear herself. As she reached the water, weighted down as she was by her heavy, silvered robes and ritual ornaments, she fought to swim away from the wreck, but the supports of the silken awning struck her and she sank below the surface.

A score of boats raced to the rescue of the high priestess, and the one which carried Morse and Laidlaw was as close as any. Morse flung off his outer garment and dived into the water. An oar struck him a glancing blow on the side of his head as he leaped, but it did not deter him. He surfaced, wiped the mingled blood and water from his eyes, and sought his direction.

The blue-and-silver awning floated thirty feet away, and there beyond it he made out a gleam of silver tissue And the clutching fingers of a hand that barely showed above the surface; then disappeared. Morse pushed himself through the water with frantic strokes, and, nearing the point where he had glimpsed the hand, he dove. Below him he saw a confused mass of garments outspread in the current, and streaming from them a mass of golden hair. He reached for the hair, seized it finally, and struggled upward. His lungs seemed about to burst before he broke the surface into the world of bright sunlight. For half a minute there was silence about him, and then a roar of excited cheers.

Morse turned on his back, paddling with his legs and one hand, letting go of the girl's hair and managing to throw his free arm about her shoulders. Leola's body, heavy with the soaked robes, dragged down, but her head was securely on his shoulder. Her face, pale as the petals of a water lily, dark eyes closed, lay turned toward his chest.

Laidlaw suddenly loomed above the couple, anchored squarely in the stern of the boat. A moment later, his powerful arms gathered in the limp form of Leola, and Morse was pulled over the side by two oarsmen.

"Row to the float!" Morse ordered gaspingly, as he fought for his breath. The sudden gale was over, and the big platform that had caused the damage had been secured. Now it swung on its broken cable, held by men in boats who had come up too late for the rescue.

Morse stepped onto the float and took Leola from Laidlaw's arms, laying her gently on the rugs and cushions that had been provided for the royal party. He knelt over her. There were no visible bruises. The support had struck the mass of her hair, tearing it from its combs and fastenings, but the thick pad of it had caused the blow to stun and not injure her. And her insensibility had prevented her from swallowing a dangerous amount of water.

As Morse knelt down, the blood from his scalp wound dropped upon her robe. He gently raised the ivory arms above her head and lowered them again to promote respiration. After a dozen motions, he was rewarded by a quiver of her eyelids and the slow, perceptible heave of her breast. Someone handed him a crystal flask, and he dropped a little of the pungent liquid between her slightly parted lips that disclosed the even, pearly teeth. Her eyes opened and gazed into his, blankly at first, before the light suddenly shone in them. She sighed.

Morse thought he distinguished some syllables and bent lower. He was not mistaken. It was his name that she murmured for a second time — not the harsh surname — but his first name, softened by the Greek tongue to "Stan-na-li." Then her eyes closed as he whispered her name in return. A faint tinge of rose appeared in her cheeks.

A group of protesting priestesses surrounded them. Two of them knelt, and Morse remembered one as the girl who had glanced up at Kiron from her litter. She pillowed Leola's head upon her lap and attempted to make her comfortable. Morse was surprised at the angry voices and glances that he drew, and allowed Laidlaw to draw him to one side where Kiron spoke to him.

"Come into my boat, both of you. You have done all you can; at least, all they'll let you do."

The barge had sunk. The priestesses had been taken in by the boats that had towed them, and they were now on the float seeking to shield their high priestess from the gaze of men.

"They seem to be angry that you saved her life," said Laidlaw, helping Morse bind a strip of linen about his head.

Kiron chuckled.

"They are," he said. "You have profaned the person of Pasiphae's representative. They will have to hold votive ceremonies for a month to wipe out the ignominy of the touch of a man. I wish I'd had your chance, though," he added ruefully.

"With Leola?" asked Laidlaw.

"Not with Leola," admitted the king. And he went on: "Rana looks furious. I watched her during the rescue and I think she sensed your anxiety. If I were you, I'd make that wound of yours an excuse for staying away from the banquet tonight. Otherwise the praise that you are bound to receive from those who do not share the priestesses' view of profanation is going to provoke Rana into a display of temper. You're not hurt are you?"

"Nothing but a scrape," replied Morse. "Sorry if I called down the wrath of Pasiphae."

But he did not look very unhappy as he said it, and Kiron rallied him.

"Leola didn't raise any objection when she revived," he said with a smile.

Morse grinned in reply. "I'll send my excuses to Rana. Laidlaw, will you take them?"

Laidlaw grunted. "You need a nurse," he said.

Later, an hour after Laidlaw had departed for the banquet, Morse rose suddenly from the lounge on which he had been lying. Strange thoughts had been running through his mind — thoughts of Leola. Since their meeting, his nature seemed to have changed, developed into a condition that left him feverish and uncertain. He had never been in love; he avoided it; he had exposed himself little to its conditions. Occasionally, when he was in New York after wanderings in little-known lands, he would find it necessary to attend some elaborate function of relatives or family friends. But here he would remain the silent, almost unseen guest, lurking in some out-of-the-way corner and dreaming of his next exploration — much to the chagrin of many of the women whose main objective seemed to be "seeing Stanley married and securely tied down."

Morse knew that he was not cut out for a life, that he was out of place in the society that bred him. But in Le-ol-a, priestess of Pasiphae, there was much to lure him. Le-ol-a, mentally alert, throwing out a challenge to men that, failing her standard, she would have none of; blessed with a beauty that was flawlessly alien to the women he knew; possessing an element of the very mystery that drew him irresistibly, time and again, to the unexplored and unknown. Leola. . .

From the first moment of meeting he had sensed the magic, the electricity between them. Now he knew what he had not seen before, hidden as it had been by this new feeling: that Leola must become his mate . . . jungle or civilization, it made no difference. And he knew, too, that he had pierced the armor of her reserve. Her eyes, the flush on her cheeks, the murmur of his name upon her lips; they told him.

But Morse did not blind himself. Rana was jealous. Leola was a priestess with vows that excluded men from her life. Love for him would expose her to a scorn — perhaps more — from the priestesses of Sele, and perhaps the virulence of Ru. Yet, if she loved him? His soul kindled at the thought. He loved her. She was the mystery that he had sought unknowingly over all the world. He would win her.

And Kiron would aid him. The king, beneath his practiced indifference, was a man, and he hid a passion for another priestess of that woman's isle. They would flee Atlantis, its intrigues and threat of revolution.

Morse's thoughts could not wait. Before him was a night of freedom. Unseen, he could slip across to the isle of Sele, forbidden though it was to men, and confront Leola in the very shrine of Pasiphae, if that were necessary.

He dressed himself with scrupulous care and lingered before the metal mirror in a fashion that would have been laughable to the Morse of a day before. It had been only twenty-four hours since he had first seen her. Since then she had looked at him with eyes that hinted at understanding and spoken with lips that had betrayed her.

He called Maya and Xolo and cautioned them to tell any inquirers that he was asleep — that he could not be disturbed. These bronzed watchmen could be relied upon in case a message came from Rana. Then he slipped away toward the water stairs.

The night was brilliant, the deserted causeway illuminated by moon and stars. The nobles were at the palace fete; the populace, tired with the day's excitement, in their homes.

Kiron had given him the key to a bronze lock that chained a light boat, and Morse stepped into it. He took up the strange, square-bladed oars and rowed the shallop swiftly from the shore, sending wavelets back along the calm surface. As the boat left the landing, two forms, clad in the tawny kilts of the priest's guard, rose from the shadow and slipped away in the direction of the palace.

Morse turned his head and saw the isle of Sele, its temple columns white beneath the moon. A bluish ray, made more conspicuous by the smoke that curled in the spreading shaft of light, lifted from behind the pillars. The lake was destitute of other craft, and an almost invisible mist hung over it in patches. Morse ran his hand through the water and was startled at the temperature. It had been warm when he rescued Leola, but now it seemed to be almost the temperature of blood.

As he approached the island, the sound of singing came to his ears. It was the chant of women's voices in a simple, pleasing harmony carried to him on the breeze. He faced the city, gray against the background of trees and cliff. The snowy cone of the volcano appeared silver, and from it came great puffs of cloud, Purple-bodied, laced at the edges by the moonlight. Morse noticed that they were on the increase from the morning.

Soon he was in the shadow of the isle. The water was deep close up to the steep and rocky shore which was thickly set with tall trees and a profusion of palms and semi-tropical under-growth. Flowers grew everywhere — on the ground — amid the shrubbery, in the treetops, and between them the vivid blossoms of orchids swung free, hanging from branches or trailing along the lianas.

Morse avoided the main landing, and paddled along easily, looking for a place to step ashore. The chanting came faintly through the trees, and above them the blue, vaporous ray showed ominously. He was aware of the danger of being discovered on the sacred island, and remembered the anger of the priestesses after his rescue of Leola. These women were trained in the use of arms, Kiron had said, and boasted of their ability to equal man in all athletic pursuits. Morse was inclined to believe in their capability. Yet, he reflected, they had screamed and shown signs of indecision in their alarm at the float. Perhaps they were unable to banish all feminine attributes.

A long, narrow cove appeared, and he headed into it silently. At its extreme the surface was covered with enormous circular leaves, the size of a table-top, among which floated huge, pink water lilies. Morse stepped ashore to a velvety turf, secured the boat, and moved through a wood in the direction of the singing. The trees were thick, and it took him a long time to make his way through the dense underbrush in the extreme darkness. Finally he broke through, and only by gripping some stout creepers did he hold himself back from a fall that would have meant instant discovery.

Morse had reached the rim of a grassy bowl that sloped before him in a sharp incline to-ward an oval of level ground at its center. The grass in the bowl was starred with gorgeous, night-blooming flowers. At one end of the oval twelve exquisitely carved columns were set in a circle. They were unroofed and unconnected and fashioned so skillfully and elaborately that they seemed to be shafts of magical growth, rather than pillars of solid stone. In the center of their circle stood an altar upon which burned the flame that formed the blue ray. Two priestesses stood beside it, one pouring oil occasionally into the reservoir that fed the flame, while the other from time to time cast into it a powder that produced the color and gave out a resinous pungent perfume.

In the open space before the shrine, a figure, clad only in a diaphanous robe, postured within a group of priestesses who lay motionless on the ground, their vestments covering them in filmy folds. Surrounding them in double ranks were the singers, waving long branches of palm in rhythm to their chant. The sound of strings and notes of piping arose from somewhere in their midst.

Brilliant moonlight illumined the scene almost as vividly as by day, yet invested it with a mystery that caused it to seem unreal, the vision of a dream.

Crouched in the thicket, his gaze fixed on the center figure whose limbs moved with exquisite grace, Morse listened to the words of the song:

"Mother of Life and Love,

Thou the All Giving Shine on us from above our faults forgiving.
Thou who divinest All our desires.
Note, as thou shinest, Thy altar fires.
Virgin and cold as we, in emulation
Strive we to copy thee with adoration.
Thy beams, descending, Enter our hearts.
Pour prayers ascending mount on our darts.
Hear us, O Pasiphae Being divine!
Smile on us, Pasiphae Shine, goddess, shine!"

The chant ended, and the prostrate votaries arose. With arms aloft, they wove in and out the measures of a stately dance about their high priestess who stood in an attitude of appeal. Her arms were extended to the moon, its beams full upon her face, subduing the pale gold of her hair to frosted silver. Faster and faster moved the dancers, their garments streaming with the pace until they formed a continuous, swiftly moving chain of shimmering silk, lowering their arms to shoulder level and linking fingers, while their naked feet seemed hardly to touch the ground.

The motion was reversed, the steps slackened, and the chain broke into separate links, each with a silent, motionless figure of supplication. The palm branches were raised moonward. The altar attendants left their fire and advanced toward Leola. From one of them she took a bow, and from the other four arrows. Impaled upon the latter, close to the points, were strips of papyrus. Leola bent the bow, and the first shaft sped upward, glittering as it curved in a graceful arc to fall beyond the rim of the basin among the trees.

The high priestess turned as she loosed one of the prayer-bearing messengers to each quarter of the heavens. The last arrow dropped within a few feet of Morse, its head buried in the turf. He reached out cautiously, secured it, and placed it within the folds of his chiton.

The altar fire was dying down. The singers and musicians had formed ranks and marched toward a path that led through the forest to their temple. The dancers followed. Only Leola remained.

When the oval was deserted, she moved slowly toward the shrine and knelt beside the altar. The flame fluttered and vanished. The high priestess regained her feet, passed her hands across her brows, then raised them toward the moon. Morse caught the sound of a faint sigh. The procession had disappeared. The words of the chant to which they marched were scarcely audible:

"Smile on us, Pasiphae!

Shine, goddess, shine!"

He cupped his hands and called softly but distinctly. "Le-ol-a!"

The high priestess started, set a swift hand to her heart, and looked toward him as he repeated her name. He stepped free of the thicket and advanced down the slope toward the shrine. She came toward him, her arms motioning him away.

"Go back!" she cried. "You must not be seen-here. It means death. Go back!"

Morse's heart gave a sudden leap. She did not want him discovered. She wanted to shield him, high priestess though she was.

"I will not go back unless you come with me," he said simply.

"With you — where?" she answered, a little wildly.

"To the edge of the forest, where your last arrow fell at my feet."

"Where my last arrow fell?" she repeated slowly, a strange look of awe upon her face.

"Yes," he insisted. "Come!"

He held out his hand, and she slipped her cool fingers into it unresistingly. Instantly he thrilled to her touch, and knew that she shared the emotion.

At the fringe of the thicket she paused and attempted to withdraw her hand.

"I must not, I will not!" she cried. "What magic have you wrought on me, O stranger?"

"Not a stranger, but 'Stan-na-li,'" he said. The moonlight could not efface the rosy color that stole into her face. "As for the magic, it was not I who used it; it was you, Leola."

"I?"

"You. For never until now did I know for what I have been seeking. As you have lived without need of man, Leola, so did I live without need of woman — until I met you. Then, as the seed breaks through the dark earth and bears a blossom, my spirit flowered. But the flower blooms only for you."

"You must not talk to me this way," she said. "I spoke to you — I came this far with you only to repay the life you saved this afternoon."

"Only for that, Leola? Swear to me that it was for that reason alone, and I will believe you and go." He forced her to meet his gaze.

"You are not kind," she murmured.

"Listen," said Morse. "I heard the words of the chant to Pasiphae."

She drew back with a gleam of anger in her eyes. "You dared — "

"I dared," he answered quietly. "And you know why I dared, Leola. It was not to witness forbidden rites. But I heard the last of the singing. You asked the moon goddess to receive the prayers impaled upon your darts. You believe that she can answer them?"

"Surely."

He took the arrow from his robe and read the linear script inscribed upon the papyrus:

"Grant, O Pasiphae, the dearest wish of our hearts."

"It fell at my feet," he said. "Your hand guided its upward flight, but surely the goddess directed its descent. Am I not the answer?"

He had dared a great deal, and resentment flamed in her glance. Then it softened.

"I do not know why I stay here talking with you," she said. "My vows — "

The moonlight faded. Clouds formed from the vapors of the volcano were being driven across the face of the planet by a breeze which was beginning to stir the tree tops in back of them.

"Look!" said Morse. "Pasiphae is mighty, but Eros conquers her and veils her face. Love has come to both of us, Leola. It spoke from our eyes as they met when the procession halted. Was it for nothing that you came ashore last night as I was being captured, for nothing that I found you in the waters of the lake and rescued you? It was the will of the gods, Leola. Fate mocks at vows, except the ones she prompts; and Fate vowed you and I to each other long ago when she willed that we should meet, though half the world divided us."

A heavy mass of vapor completely shrouded the moon and chased the watchful shadows. Morse placed his arms about her and drew her to him. For a moment she resisted, then suddenly accepted the embrace. Her face was lifted slowly to his, as if fighting against surrender. He set his palm against the masses of her hair and bent his lips to her. They were tremulous, but warm with life, and met his in a kiss that joined them irrevocably.

Men broke through the undergrowth, seized Morse from behind, and tore Leola from his arms. Her hair caught upon a trailing vine and showered down in a rain of pale gold as the moon's disk cleared. Morse struggled in silence as more men flung themselves upon him, but Leola shook off the lighter grasp of the two that held her.

"How dare you!" she gasped. "How dare you! One cry and my followers will come and slay you for your profanation!"

A man took a step from the band. He was bearded and dressed in priestly vestments. Morse recognized him as one of Ru's advisers.

"You have no followers, Leola," he said sternly. "It is you who have profaned your own shrine. Do you think the priestesses of Pasiphae will obey one who has forsworn her vows and brought the worship of the goddess into disrepute?"

Leola was silenced. Rude hands were clapped across Morse's mouth before he could prevent it. The next moment he was trussed and helpless, and being carried to the cove where he had landed. Beside his shallop was a galley manned by slaves. He was tossed into its stern like a bundle, and the next moment Leola, also bound and gagged, was laid beside him.

Morse was sick at the thought of what he had brought upon the woman he loved, and he twisted until the hide strips sank into his flesh. His arm rested against Leola's, and her fingers interlaced themselves in his with a pressure that was forgiveness perhaps, perhaps love.

The galley was poled out of the cove, and under lusty strokes raced toward the mainland. As Morse lay there, the wind lifted a fragrant tress of Leola's hair, and it fell across his face like a caress. He touched it with his lips.

The boat glided against the landing, and the prisoners were lifted out silently and carried up the water stairs. Morse saw the cone of the volcano lifting its peak against the stars, its hoary crest gleaming frostily. The puffs of vapor had turned into an uninterrupted flow of smoke that funneled out to a dense mass, part of which streamed leeward like a dusty, pointing finger. The lower part of the cloud was tinged with a lurid, pulsating glow.

The palace festival hall was a blaze of light as the prisoners were ushered in. Its tables were arranged in a wide U, and the diners had apparently rearranged their places in expectation of something to come. Ru sat by the side of Rana, and back of them were ranged the priests of Minos. The guard was heavily disposed inside the door.

Morse looked around, first for Kiron and then for Laidlaw, but both men were absent.

Morse and Leola had been placed upon their feet outside the entrance, their lower bonds loosened in order that they might walk, and then forced into the dining hall by their captors. Rana regarded them with the eyes of a basilisk, and Ru with more complacency but none the less assurance.

"So, my sister," said Rana fiercely, "it seems that you are more human than we thought. You — the woman who styled the other sex stupid — have succumbed to the seduction of a stranger."

Leola surveyed the queen calmly, as if she had not spoken, and Ru took up the denunciation.

"Priestess of Pasiphae, you are forsworn," he said, and the nobles about the tables craned their necks to listen. "The fire mountain shows the anger of the gods. The lake itself is an emblem of their growing wrath. We have consulted the oracles with anxious questionings, and they have answered."

In the silence that fell upon the hall as Ru paused, the heavy breathing of the audience betrayed their fear and superstition. Ru looked at them with the air of an animal trainer who had been doubtful whether his performers had forgotten their tricks, but now he knew that they were held well in hand.

"The oracle has said: 'From fire and water was Atlantis born. When fire and water mingle, then the beginning shall be the end. Watch carefully, lest destruction come from without. Desert not the gods, lest in time of peril they in turn desert you.'

"'When fire and water mingle!' The lake will soon begin to boil unless the danger can be averted. Vapor hangs over it tonight — vapor born of the mingling of the elements. 'Watch carefully, lest destruction come from without.' Within our midst, in the very center of our age-old worship of the eternal gods — Leola has been unfaithful to her vows, a priestess who has flouted the gods and made a mockery of them before their own altars!"

A muttering broke out along the line of tables. Rana alone said nothing, but she bent a venomous gaze upon her sister who looked through her as if she had not been present.

"From the outside have come strangers with talk of peoples who are so much more powerful than Atlantis. If they are so great and wise, why do they come to spy upon us? Why are they not content to remain in their own land as we are in Atlantis? Yet, we would have treated them courteously, but they have conspired with this recreant priestess to pollute our sacred shrines. Their penalty must be death!"

The mutterings grew louder, but under Ru's piercing stare no one dared show signs of dissent.

"And simple death cannot atone for, nor avert, the gathering displeasure of the gods. Sacrifice alone will appease them!"

A slight tremor rocked the building, and the lamps swung on the chains that supported them. Ru's eyes blazed with triumph.

"See!" he cried. "The gods answer and accept!"

The mutterings changed to audible exclamations of awe and wonder. Into the faces of the nobles, men and women alike, crept the look that they had worn in the amphitheater. Their eyes hardened and their mouths grew cruel. There had been no human sacrifices in Atlantis for some time; it would be a rare spectacle.

"The false priestess shall stand upon the Spot of Sacrifice while Re touches with his shining finger the rays of his emblem," said Ru. "As for the stranger, let him learn the embrace of the Bull of Minos."

Morse, wondering what horrors might lie in the fate decreed for Leola, dimly sensed what his own would be. He knew the ancient torture of the Minoans described in the frescoes of Cnossus, where strangers were "presented" to the bull, shut up within the belly of a brazen image made red-hot to receive them. Doomed and without hope as he believed them, strangely, death seemed far away, unfathomable. His mind was misty, and idly, without feeling, he wondered what they would do to Laidlaw, and if the scientist had already been condemned.

Dimly he heard the thrill, almost the pleasure, in the tones of the nobles as they repeated: "The Bull of Minos!"

He turned to Leola, and her eyes held an open avowal of love before they saddened to farewell.

"Forgive me," he said hoarsely. The mist was clearing from his mind as the hands of the guards took hold of him.

"There is nothing to forgive," Leola answered quietly. "You have given me love, and that is more than life!"

"Silence, you wanton!" It was the shrill voice of Rana, cracking in its malignity and unsuppressed anger. The queen had risen, and her face was convulsed with a deadly hatred. Ru laid a restraining hand upon her arm.

Leola smiled. "Yours is a hollow victory, my sister. I win far more than I lose, and you lose what you could never have won."

Rana snatched a sharp-cutting dagger from the table and threw it with all her strength and fury. Hate thwarted her aim, and the blade sank into the shoulder of a guard who stood close by.

Ru motioned the captives away.

There was a sudden rush of sandaled feet, and the hall was filled with the indignant priestesses of Pasiphae. Their heads were topped with crested helmets, their waists girdled with swords. Some carried long shields that covered their bodies and bore spears, while the remainder were armed with bows and arrows. They surrounded Leola, the feathered shafts threatening Rana and Ru. The guards fell back sullenly; the determination of these women warriors was not to be held lightly.

One of the two priestesses who had been carried abreast of Leola in the afternoon procession — it was not the girl who had glanced at Kiron — advanced halfway the length of the tables and addressed Ru.

"By what right," she demanded, in a tone of arrogance and anger, "do your guards seize the person of our high priestess upon the isle of Sele, within the holy borders of the shrine?"

Ru answered evenly:

"The priests of Minos have always held the right of entry upon Sele. But wait — " he cried, as the priestess started to bring up her spear. "Hear me out. We followed in the footsteps of this stranger, believing that he intended to violate the sacred precincts of the isle to keep a tryst with Leola."

There was a movement of disbelief, of repulsion, among the priestesses, and their gaze fastened on Leola's face.

"We found her," continued Ru, "in his embrace. She cannot deny it. Ask her," he cried, as the priestesses protested in indignation.

The spokeswoman turned to Leola, half-fearfully. The unasked question was in her silent glance.

"It is true," the high priestess admitted calmly.

As swiftly as waves retreat from a sloping beach, the priestesses of Pasiphae drew back from Leola as a thing abhorred, whose touch would befoul them. Only one remained close to her; it was the one whom Kiron had called Lycida. She hesitated for a moment as the others moved away sullenly. Then she stepped to Leola's side, lifting her head fearlessly, and checked the high priestess before she could speak.

"Then I, too," she said, looking scornfully at her fellows, "abjure my vows. My respect for her is stronger than my devotion to Pasiphae. The vows of friendship to flesh and blood are stronger than those to a goddess in the souls of whose followers humanity is as lifeless as the flame that died last night upon the altar of the shrine."

Her voice rang out fearlessly, and her dark eyes flashed.

"So be it," said Ru grimly. "You have cast your lot with flesh and blood, and your fate is entwined with the fate of Leola. The gods will appreciate another offering. Tomorrow, at dawn, you may have cause for regret when you face an offended Pasiphae at the entrance of the underworld."

Lycida shivered, but stood as straight as an arrow.

"We will give them into your keeping," continued Ru to the priestesses. "We will await you in the Hall of Sacrifice an hour before sunrise."

It was a shrewd move that allied the irate votaries of Pasiphae with him in the judgment that he had declared. He had no wish to offend them at the present. There was time enough for that later on.

The first priestess, whose eyes already held a look of satisfied ambition, hesitated for only a moment. At a sign from her, the armed priestesses closed in about Leola and her companion and led them from the hall.

The sound of their departure had barely died away when there was a noise of confusion in the antechamber. The clang of a shield, the quick clatter of weapons, and the imperious voice of Kiron ordered the guards to stand aside.

A little phalanx of nobles entered, swords in hand. They were armored in helmets, breastplates, and greaves, and their sword arms were protected from wrist to elbow by plates of bronze. With them were the personal attendants of the young king, the Indians Maya and Xolo who flanked Laidlaw, and Kiron himself. The scientist and the two Indians held rifles. Thrusting the guards aside, they surrounded Morse, their shields welded into an unbreakable barrier.

"This time, Ru, you have usurped your prerogatives," said Kiron. "This man and this" — he indicated Morse and Laidlaw — "can hardly be called strangers. On the contrary, they are citizens and nobles of Atlantis, members of the Brotherhood of Kol, epoptae and mystae of the ritual over which you presided. They can be judged only by the will of the people."

Ru's face grew scarlet, and the veins on his forehead stood out as if he had been lashed.

"This we will not countenance!" he shrieked. "Our shrines have been profaned. Their lives are forfeit. Be careful that you do not involve yourself!"

He struck a gong that hung upon a tripod close by him. Above its sound broke a heavy detonation, and again the palace shook to its foundations.

"Listen to the voice of Minos," cried Ru. "Atlantis is shaken. We lie in the hollow of his palm. Beware or he will close it and crush us."

In answer to the sound of the gong, a company of guards appeared behind Ru to strengthen his position. Consternation reigned among the feasters. The violence of the tremor and the ferocity of Ru's speech frightened them, and the priest was quick to recognize this. The terror of the moment had invested him with all the ancient powers of his office.

"Seize them!" he cried, and the guards rushed at the little force who stood firm to the attack, outnumbered though they were. A clash of bronze upon bronze sounded as Kiron and his men fiercely resisted the crush of men who sought to cut them down by shear weight of numbers.

Morse and Laidlaw, joined by Maya and Xolo, forced their way into the front ranks, and opened fire, the first use of firearms that the Atlanteans had ever witnessed. The noise of the rifles and automatics was almost lost in the fierce combat, but Ru's guards saw the spitting fire and shrank back before the stream of lead that smashed through flesh and bone and left a dozen of their number on the floor.

Morse caught a glimpse of the head and shoulders of Ru behind the mass of guards, and he fired without taking aim. The bullet smashed against the golden headpiece that the high priest wore and sent it banging to the floor. Ru bobbed low with surprising alacrity and kept out of sight behind his guards.

"Quickly!" shouted Kiron, as the attack slackened. "Before they can cut us off."

Still facing their opponents, the little band backed slowly through the door and then hastened along the corridor to Kiron's quarters. A few of the party had been wounded in the short conflict, and these were treated as Kiron revealed his doings to the Americans.

"I sent a messenger to your apartments and learned from the Indians that you had left instructions not to be disturbed. After a little while Ru was interrupted by some of his men who talked excitedly, although I could not hear what was said. An evil but satisfying look came over his face as he exchanged a word with Rana, and then his men rushed off with new instructions.

"As soon as the opportunity presented itself, I slipped away to your apartments. Maya admitted that you were not there, and I set out to find you. The boat that I had lent you was gone, and a little distance from there I found a fisherman who told me of an incoming barge that held prisoners from Sele. Messages were sent to Laidlaw and these men whom I felt certain I could count on, and we armed ourselves. You know the rest. What do you know of Leola?"

Morse told him and the king's face became pale and hard as he heard of the devotion of the priestess, Lycida.

"They left the palace by another way," he said slowly. "If I had met them. . ." he paused and let his sentence go unfinished, fighting deep emotion. Finally he gained control of himself.

"We cannot stay here indefinitely. The doors are solid, but Ru will inflame all of Atlantis against us. They are already in mortal fear from the earth tremors. The fisherman told me that the western waters are white with dead fish, and the paint on his boat was blistered with the heat. The volcanic cloud is red with the reflection of fire."

He turned to the nobles who had fought for him. "I do not wish to embroil you in this quarrel, my friends. Yet, I am afraid that you are already marked men."

"Your cause is ours, Kiron," one of them answered for all.

"Good! If I can get word to my villa, there are fifty men there who are well-trained in the use of arms. But our numbers will still remain too few," he mused sadly.

"Leola and her friend must be rescued," interposed Morse quietly but firmly. "Ru plans to sacrifice them at dawn. We must reach them somehow. A raid on Sele — "

"We would be cut down before we reached the boats," said Kiron.

"Then a bold stroke in the temple. Can you gain us entrance somehow? If we could hide ourselves until the right moment, seize the girls, and fight out way to the tunnel, we might have a chance. The guns will hold them off if we can take them by surprise."

Kiron looked at Morse doubtfully.

"It is the only thing we can do," he agreed finally. "It is a desperate chance. Your death tubes may aid us to win through, but I think Ru will be certain to guard the tunnel. But I can gain access to the temple by the royal entrance. It opens only to my touch, and even Ru does not have the secret. The passage leads from here to the chamber of Tele, the astrologer. He will help us, for he has no love for Ru. The priests hate him because he will not read the stars to suit their will."

A fierce hammering sounded on the metal doors that shut off the wing from the rest of the palace. Maya appeared to tell them that Ru's forces had mustered for an attack.

"If the doors will hold them for awhile, " said Morse, "we can collect our ammunition and make our way to your astrologer."

On the outside, men battered savagely at the doors. It took only a few moments to secure the arms, the flashlights, and the field glasses. They stepped into the large room that housed the king's pool, and Kiron moved to its side, reaching for some unseen object beneath the water's surface. There was a rush of water, and the pool emptied rapidly.

Kiron turned and motioned them down a flight of steps.

Along the side of the pool, a series of bronze rings were set for handholds. The king inspected them carefully, selected one, and gave it a peculiar twist to the side. A low door appeared, and they passed through, followed by the nobles who had cast their lot with the king. The passage was pitch dark. Laidlaw switched on his flashlight and by its light Kiron found a lever set in the wall. As he pulled it, the door behind them closed quickly, and the sound of water was easily distinguishable. The pool was being refilled.

"The doors should hold them," said Kiron hopefully. "I made sure that they were well built. By the time they have them down, the pool will have reached its normal level. Let me lead. There are other tricks that make this hidden way secure."

CHAPTER XII
THE HALL OF SACRIFICE

The hidden way led downward with sudden dips and turns. Along the route they passed through two ancient doors, both several inches thick and encased in metal. They were opened only after Kiron had spoken through a tube and set in motion delicately balanced machinery that was controlled by the action of a diaphragm. Finally, they came to the end of the passage — to face a blank wall.

Silencing his companions, Kiron blew into a pipe that ran into the wall. For a minute nothing happened, and then a soft, muffled whistle penetrated back through the tube. Laidlaw and Morse exchanged glances as Kiron spoke swiftly into the tube and stepped back. The wall slid silently away, and they crowded into a room that was almost filled by the numbers of their party.

An old man, bowed nearly double, so that his straggling beard swept the floor, greeted them. The men of the king's party moved a step backward, involuntarily, awed to be in the presence of the astrologer who could read in the stars the secrets of their life and death.

The stargazer wore a black robe emblazoned with rayed disks worked in gold and silver. On his breast was the representation of the sun, centered by an opal that changed color at every laboring breath. His hands shook palsiedly. The wrinkled skin of his face held the unhealthy pallor of shadowed fungi. Only his two eyes lived, and they mated the opal of the ornament.

His first words halted the king's speech. "I expected you, Kiron," he said simply, in a deep voice that was astonishingly vibrant. "You and the strangers. The stars have told me." He pointed to a circular stone on which was engraved a mass of symbols.

"In the month of Pasiphae, in this generation, disaster shall come to Atlantis. Disaster from within and without. The appointed time is here. As the stars are born in flame and perish in dead ashes, so nations rise and fall as the gods have appointed.

"Still, the children of Atlantis will not perish in entirety. In an alien land, you" — he pointed a wavering finger at Kiron — "will survive with the priestess you love. In the far days to come, your son's son shall once again rule the people of Minos. And you" — he fixed his lustrous eyes upon a fascinated Morse — "you, too shall breed those who will restore the ancient glory of Atlantis.

"Last night, I read the Stars. Soon you will travel beneath constellations I have never seen; yet ones I know well. You will tread a path laid out aeons before you drew your first breath. I have prophesized this to Ru and his priests, but because I have refused to twist the inexorable law that is written in the sky to their ambitions, I am discredited.

"What is your will?"

Kiron explained quickly, and the sage nodded.

"Rest in the best manner that you can until I call you," he said. "I go to read the symbols of the night. No one will suspect your presence here. Will you come with me, man of another land?" he asked Laidlaw. "My time is short, and yet I would exchange knowledge with you. The brain may die, but knowledge is incorruptible. When we return I will place you behind the calendar disk in a hollow that is unknown to Ru. The disk is pierced in its carving, and you can observe all that passes, and at the chosen moment enter the temple.

"The way is difficult, and the omens tell of hardship and death. Yet courage will take you to your end."

Laidlaw and the astrologer disappeared up a narrow, winding stair, and the party relaxed as far as cramped quarters would permit. There could be no thought of sleep in the anxiety of what was to come,: and presently Kiron arose.

"The way should be clear now," he said. "I will return to my quarters by the way that we entered, and then leave the palace in disguise. We can use the men who are at my villa. I think the tunnel to the outer world will be guarded, but there is an old exit at the northern end of the lake that was closed many years ago. Still, we may be able to open it — if we can get that far."

Morse tried to dissuade him, but the king was resolute.

"We must have more men," he said, and Morse reluctantly acknowledged this. Even with the advantage given them by their firearms, they would be smothered quickly by the sheer weight of the numbers opposing them.

Kiron departed, and the moments dragged until Tele and Laidlaw returned.

"There are two hours left before daylight," said Laidlaw, "and the night is almost as bright as day with the reflection from the volcano. Unless I miss my guess, we're going to see an eruption within twenty-four hours. We counted four shocks while we were on the parapet, and the city is beginning to awaken. Ru has sent messengers out to keep the people informed."

"Damn him!" said Morse. "I won't miss the next time I get a shot at him. Did you see anything of Kiron?"

"We didn't see him, and we were careful not to expose ourselves," said Laidlaw, once Morse had explained the king's errand. "There are many boats on the lake. The priestesses from Sele have arrived, and we heard them chanting."

Aside to Morse, he said: "Tele has cast his lot with us. By giving us sanctuary he will be linked to us the moment we show ourselves from behind the calendar stone. He is a rare mixture of shrewdness and more than a smattering of real science. I hope we can take him back with us. I like him. You haven't brought anything along to eat, have you?"

"Not I," Morse answered. "Didn't you satisfy yourself at the feast?"

"My mouth was filled with words when it should have been full of meat," said Laidlaw wryly.

"I'm afraid you'll be long hungry before our next meal. We've got to be moving."

They filed down a slanting corridor to find themselves in a circular chamber closed by a great circle of stone slitted with deep carving on its unexposed side. The flashlight showed a bronze pipe that was fitted with a mouthpiece leading to a box-like affair above the stone.

"Tele's private megaphone by which he spouts his oracles," guessed Laidlaw. He switched off his flashlight at the astrologer's directive.

They crowded around the openings that looked into the Hall of Sacrifice. The darkness harbored them, and they waited, fingering their weapons nervously.

Suddenly, lights appeared in the inner chamber. The hall was revealed in all its vastness, a forbidding place carved from solid rock. Frescoes of frightening sacrificial rites decorated the walls. Directly in line with the calendar stone was an altar, a high platform built of massive blocks on which rested a golden flower, its petals closed upon its center. Above it loomed the savage figure of the deity, cross-legged, clad in a loin cloth, a mighty idol with the head of a bull. Its eyes glowed crimson, and one hand held a torch that spouted a flame of natural gas. The other held a golden goblet. Steps led up to the altar, and on either side stood two thrones of marble.

A murmur of voices reached the ears of the hidden people. Before them Ru and his attendants entered the chamber and prostrated themselves before the altar. They were clad in ceremonial vestments that fairly coruscated with gems and polished metal.

Morse's finger itched on the trigger of his pistol. Only the knowledge that a shot would destroy all chances of saving Leola restrained him.

A priest advanced to a pillar that was hewn in rough semblance of a human figure with bowed shoulders that supported the roof of the chamber. He pressed a center spot in the carved figure. Slowly the petals of the flower lifted and fell back until they formed the rays of the sun about a transparent center of crystal through which shone a ruddy glow. Another man worked a lever from behind one of the thrones. A grating noise could be heard; Ru and the priests stepped rapidly aside as a portion of floor opened before them, and the chamber was filled with the glare and heat of a roaring furnace, Tongues of fierce flame increased the temperature perceptibly before the opening closed again.

"The Spot of Sacrifice," whispered Laidlaw. "Connected by a shaft with the volcano itself, I think. At dawn, the sun shines through a crack that penetrates the roof and faces the east. The is the finger of Minos which stirs his emblem, the sun flower, to life. With its opening the shaft is uncovered, and the victim is shot into the incandescent lava.

"Of course the sunbeam is a theatrical trick. The devilish invention works mechanically. But the finger of Minos is a vital part of the ritual that ties it to the supernatural. And Tele declares it will not pierce the slit today, though there is no eclipse due. He thinks the smoke from the volcano will veil the sun, and he's probably right. It should put a hitch in Ru's ceremonial."

"I hope so," said Morse anxiously. "I'm afraid something may have happened to Kiron. He's got to be here before daylight to do us any good or to avoid discovery."

Ru and his followers, satisfied that the hellish machine was in working order, departed. The lights still burned in the Hall of Sacrifice, and from beyond the walls the silent watchers could hear the faint sound of chanting.

After a time, a column of guards filed in and fixed ropes to keep back the populace who were never allowed too close to the "divine" mysteries. When this was completed, some of the men took up stations by the main entrance, and the crowd swarmed in. Their murmur of conversation was subdued in the presence of the god and the nature of the circumstance.

Finally, Ru and his train made their entrance. In another part of the chamber, a door opened, and the sound of chanting became clear and loud. The priestesses of Pasiphae, their white and silver vestments changed for robes of somber purple that was almost a black marched toward the altar. In their midst Leola and Lycida walked with heads erect.

Four of the priests received the victims, as the priestesses took up a station to the right of the altar, standing opposite to the attendants of Ru. There was a long pause.

In the cavity behind the calendar stone, Morse and Laidlaw could hear the beating of their hearts as they prayed for Kiron's coming. They counted a double company of guards within the Hall of Sacrifice, and another detachment entered in company with Rana, who passed by Leola with a look of triumph. She seated herself majestically on one of the thrones, while the other — the throne of Kiron — remained empty.

The priests of Minos began a sacred song to the sun. Ru stood in an expectant attitude, glancing above him to the cut in the roof through which the sunbeam would fall. The four priests bound the feet of the victims, and Leola was left standing on the Spot of Sacrifice.

At Tele's bidding, the little company grouped to one side behind the calendar stone. The astrologer readied himself to touch the mechanism that would swing the stone on a pivot, watching Morse intently. Morse, in turn, watched every move of the priests for the first suggestion of a movement that would cause the flower to open.

But Ru cast anxious looks at the slot above him. The lights had been lowered to make the appearance of the sunbeam more effective, but nothing happened. Twice the priests repeated the final phrases of their chant:

"The Sun God comes in flame.
    Hail unto Re, all hail!
    Acclaim his sacred name To Re, all hail!"

No finger of light appeared. The people shifted uneasily, and a deep voice sounded:
    "Re refuses the sacrifice.
    He shines not upon deeds that are unjust."

It was the voice of the Oracle. For a moment even Ru was startled. Morse could see the frightened eyes of the guards as Tele's impressive voice boomed through his megaphone. He had confided the secret of the sunbeam's non-appearance. The earthquake had loosened courses from the roof, but, with characteristic mystery, reserved this knowledge until it became necessary to use every second of delay.

Ru grew furious, aware that his own tricks were being used against him. He faced the people knowing that he must act without delay.

"By Re and Minos," he cried, "the Oracle speaks falsely. The sun is veiled by the smoke from the volcano. But its power can pierce the cloud. Look! The sun flower opens!"

A priest had moved silently to the pillar and touched the hidden stud. The rays began to lift. A second priest advanced toward the lever that would precipitate Leola into the shaft as the heart of the flower was disclosed.

The calendar stone revolved on its edge, and Morse, Laidlaw, and their band swept into the temple. Laidlaw fired at the priest, who dodged unhurt behind Rana's throne as soon as he caught sight of them. Morse caught Leola to his side, while Rana, maddened by rage and jealousy, leaped at her sister with an upraised knife. From behind the throne Ru cried out to stop her, but the queen gave him not so much as a look. At that moment a portion of the floor rolled back, and a great tongue of flame shot almost to the temple roof. Rana shrieked, dropped her weapon, and covered her face with her hands, seared and blinded with the leaping flames. She tottered and fell forward with a hideous shriek into the shaft of death.

The temple became a bedlam. The guards fell back momentarily, then attacked the band with fury, pressing them back toward the calendar stone. Suddenly, Kiron appeared behind them with a body of fifty men, and the guards fell back before these new reinforcements. The king moved forward swiftly and pulled Lycida from the arms of a pair of Ru's henchmen who had sought to push her into the flames.

For a moment, there was a lull in the fighting, and then Ru's strong voice called out. He urged the multitude to avenge their queen and the profanation of the temple, and the spectators, who had been silent spectators to the fierce battle, looked at each other dumbly. Ru's urging was renewed, and then with a thunderous roar the mob surged forward. Morse had time to set Leola behind the stone, and then joined Laidlaw and the two Indians in a fusillade at their attackers. But the wave could not be stopped; the numbers were too great.

Tele was down, gasping his life away with a great wound in his breast. And Kiron himself was hard pressed until Laidlaw, noticing the king's peril, shot two of his closest adversaries. Ru, his passion kindled by the overpowering rush of the multitude, forgot his danger in the impending victory. He moved from his sanctuary behind the throne, shrieking his hate. And for just a moment he was revealed to Morse.

The American steadied himself and his aim was true. A crimson star blazed on the forehead of the high priest, and he screamed, spun wildly, and plunged headlong into the fiery pit.

In the next minute the band was behind the great stone, and Kiron fumbled for the hidden spring. He found it, and the ponderous mass shut out the furious attackers.

CHAPTER XIII

THE END OF ATLANTIS

For what seemed like hours, but what was in reality only a few minutes, Kiron and his companions traversed unused passages until they had reached the street. As they emerged from the palace, the earth shook violently, and a number of men were thrown to the ground. The sky was leaden where the great pall of the volcano shifted above the city, lit up by sudden flashes. The lake was covered with waves in which fish floated by the thousands, and steam hung above the surface like a low fog.

Here and there along the causeway sections of cornices had fallen. Apparently tremors, which had gone unnoticed in the low level of the temple during the intense fighting, had been occurring with greater frequency.

Kiron led them to the boats in which he had landed his men. As the band showed themselves on the main causeway, howls of rage greeted them. Behind them, they saw the first ranks of the infuriated populace, some of the guards, and a few of the bolder priests, who burst from the temple entrance like angry hornets.

The boats were boarded and pushed into the lake with less than a hundred feet to spare, but the pursuers poured into other vessels, and their oars lashed the water to a frenzied foam. Morse, Laidlaw, and the two Indians sought to discourage them with their rifles, but the odds were too great. And many of the pursuing craft, with two tiers of oars, were gradually overhauling them.

"We'll have to land on Sele," shouted Kiron. "We can fight them from the water stairs and have the temple to fall back to."

"We'll have to watch out or they'll flank us," said Morse, remembering the cove. "Are there any other landing places besides that one they used to capture us?" he asked Leola.

"There are none," she answered.

"Then Maya and Xolo can guard the cove with a dozen men and their guns. If only we had more rifles!"

The little group moved away quickly, following the Indians. There was little time for talk, barely time to range themselves upon the shallow steps of Sele, before the leading galley moved alongside, and the fight was on again.

Morse and Laidlaw checked the first attack, but ammunition was running low. Moreover, their opponents were now fully convinced that the volcanic eruption and earthquake were caused by the actions of the priestess and the outsiders, and they fought desperately. Soon, the lower steps were covered with dead and dying, but the attack did not waver. Step by step the little force retreated, fighting tenaciously. Behind shields set edge to edge, they wielded their swords, while those in the second line flung short javelins or thrust with long spears.

The defenders held the advantage of the steps which had been hewn from the rocky bed of the island. Yet, they were rolled back inevitably toward the temple. Three galleys had landed, and in the distance additional ships were leaving the city.

The guards, trained fighters that they were, fought like fiends. Their giant leader appeared invulnerable as he swung his ax with frightful and deadly dexterity, changing it to either hand as the occasion demanded and shouting wild cries to which his henchmen responded. Kiron attacked him and was beaten to his knees, recovering under the prompt covering of friendly shields.

At last the little band of defenders found themselves unable to retreat — they had been backed against the columns of the temple. Laidlaw and Morse were close beside each other when they fired their last cartridges. Morse stooped to secure a spear, and, as he rose, the giant guardsman, cleaving a way through the wavering ranks, charged at him. His swift leap evaded Morse's spearthrust, and with a shout of triumph he leaped in, ax swinging high. Morse was off-balance, and there was no aid at hand. Laidlaw was throttling an assailant in his powerful hands, and the balance of Kiron's men were reeling in near-exhaustion. Before Morse could ready himself for a defense, something whistled past his ear. The giant guardsman, with a look of astonishment, dropped his ax and flung up both arms.

From his broad chest protruded the feathered shaft of an arrow. Others began to fly, two in a volley, straight to their marks. Morse secured the bronze battleax that had threatened him and turned to see Leola and her companion, Lycida, loosing arrow after arrow against their attackers. There were no bows to be used in retaliation. The weapon had become almost obsolete and was used only by the priestesses of Pasiphae as a sacred symbol.

Morse waved at Leola, and she called out encouragement. Laidlaw had found a sword and was swinging it around him with unquenchable fury, the great scientist lost in a berserk madness. Morse, ax in hand, fought to his side, and together they inspired a rally that drove back the attackers. As the fighting ceased, Maya and Xolo came up on the run, followed closely by the men who had been dispatched to guard the other landing. They reported that an earthquake had closed the cove, squeezing the rocks into a high dike. These reinforcements were welcome, particularly the weapons with the few remaining cartridges.

But it could only be the beginning of the end. Less than a dozen of the initial force remained on their feet. The survivors were wounded, bruised, almost too weary to lift their weapons. Twenty boats were on the lake, bringing certain death closer at every oar pull.

In the breathing space by fate they greeted each other with grim smiles. The two priestesses stood close to the men they had chosen over their vows, and Laidlaw surveyed them with looks of kindly sympathy. The scientist looked like a Viking warrior, with his hair and beard in a ruffled mane. Bare from the waist, his body was splotched with blood, and there was a nasty cut on one forearm. He had set a helmet on his head, and a gory sword was still clutched in one hand.

"It's a good way to go out," he grinned. "I've always thought I'd like to be in one good, smashing fight. And we've had it. Ey! Here they come!"

The lovers embraced for a final time. The flotilla was less than a hundred yards away, and shouts of vengeance carried from them. The three galleys that had first pursued them floated idly, covered with dead and dying, a monument to the bravery of the hunted. But less than twenty remained able to give battle to an enemy numbering more than a thousand.

A frightful roar came from the volcano. The cloud pall shook and scattered as flame shot up. The crater lip became a molten mass that slowly moved down the steep slopes, erasing the snow. The island quivered, shook. Behind them temple columns toppled and crashed down. The water stairs were split in two, the edges grinding and working hungrily against each other. A great wave suddenly slapped at the land and sent its scalding spray among them. The men in the boats ceased to row. A second lava overflow spilled from the crater in time with a second shock.

Leola clutched at Morse's arm.

"Look!" she cried, pointing to the northern shore. The wall of the lake was opening! The mountain dissolved before their eyes, a great wedge splitting below the water line. Clouds of fine ash began to fall, covering the lake with scum and the land with fine powder that choked them., The boats were now rowing frantically for the farther shore.

"They'll never make it," said Laidlaw. "The current will grip them. They'll go over that Niagara — listen to the sound of it. The lake's emptying! Damn these ashes; my mouth's full of them!"

They climbed the shattered steps and entered the half-ruined temple. Leola led them to an inner chamber where they found food and drink. And somehow they ate by the light of a pair of torches. The temple lights had been destroyed, and the sifting ashes turned the day to a choking twilight. The volcanic dust became unbearable, and they descended into the temple crypts, where flashlight rays exposed rows of skeletons in niches hollowed from the rock.

Laidlaw examined the latter.

"Lava," he said. "The whole island's built out of it. These tunnels are of volcanic formation. I'm afraid that we and Atlantis are going to go out together."

Morse took Leola in his arms. "Are you afraid?" he asked.

"Afraid? Of what? No matter where the path leads, we go down it together."

"I believe we'll get clear," said Kiron optimistically. "Do you remember Tele's prediction? That with courage we would win through? I have faith in that last Oracle of his. He was generally too correct to be popular."

Encouraged by Kiron, they fought the hours in silence. No ashes reached them, but the air grew foul and hot. Twice earth tremors of lessening violence loosened ancient skeletons upon them. Gradually the temperature increased until they could endure it no longer.

"Lava rising in the old channels," announced Laidlaw. "But the shocks seem to have ended. Suppose we take a look."

The world on which they gazed was new to them. The wan rays of the setting sun shone tired and old upon a gray landscape. The volcanic ash had ceased to fall, but everywhere there was a fine dust — uprooted trees, damaged buildings, all powdered to the same dreary shade. The water stairs — what was left of them — ended in a sheer drop to what had been the lake. The water had fallen thirty feet, and the turbid current swirled slowly toward the gap in the mountains through which it still poured with the noise of a distant cataract. There was not a boat to be seen.

The city of Dor stood upon cliffs. Many of its buildings had fallen, and its palace and temple were on fire. Little remained that had escaped nature's hand of destruction. Nor was there any sign of human survival. The volcano vomited its pall of smoke, black above, blood-red below, and the slow lava stream had almost reached the line of trees. Everything was dull with the gray film that floated in patches upon the dying lake. Here was the abomination of desolation.

"Not a cheerful outlook," said Morse. "But it is an outlook!"

"There are no boats," said Kiron.

"There are trees," Morse answered. "We can build a raft."

Three months later there was talk across the table in Morse's dining room.

"I think I'll go back to Atlantis," said Laidlaw. Kiron made a face. "Haven't you had enough of destruction?" he asked.

Laidlaw smiled. "I don't think you four have been married long enough for me to coax away the grooms, but I want to finish my researches, and with Kiron's permission I'm going to form a company."

"A company for what?" asked Kiron. "And why with my permission?"

"Because you should have the first claim on it. The lake bottom off the temple water stairs ought to be high and dry by now. There's a fortune lying there in gold and jewels to be picked up."

"Getting a mercenary streak, Laidlaw?" laughed Morse.

"Money is always useful, if only to leave to godchildren," answered the scientist. "I'll use most of it for archeological researches, with the exception of the possible legacies just mentioned. Want to come with me, Kiron?"

The late king of Atlantis shook his head.

"We haven't started on what you call our honeymoon yet. Better come with us, Laidlaw. We are going to spend it in Crete."

"A lot of company you'd be to me, or I to you," said the scientist. "I prefer Atlantis. How about you, Morse? Think of the treasure-trove we can uncover."

"I think," said Morse, as his hand closed over that of Leola's, "that as far as I'm concerned, I have the treasure of Atlantis."

THE END